AUGUST BLUE

By the same author

Ophelia and the Great Idea
Beautiful Mutants
Swallowing Geography
The Unloved
Diary of a Steak
Billy & Girl
Pillow Talk in Europe and Other Places
Swimming Home
Black Vodka
Things I Don't Want to Know
Hot Milk
The Cost of Living
The Man Who Saw Everything
Real Estate

AUGUST BLUE

Deborah Levy

HAMISH HAMILTON
an imprint of
PENGUIN BOOKS

HAMISH HAMILTON

UK | USA | Canada | Ireland | Australia
India | New Zealand | South Africa

Hamish Hamilton is part of the Penguin Random House group of companies
whose addresses can be found at global.penguinrandomhouse.com.

First published 2023
001

Copyright © Deborah Levy, 2023

Epigraph on p. v excerpted from *My Mother Laughs* by Chantal Akerman,
translated by Daniella Shreir and published by Silver Press, 2019.
Reproduced by permission of the publisher

The moral right of the author has been asserted

Set in 14.25/18.75pt Fournier MT Pro
Typeset by Jouve (UK), Milton Keynes
Printed and bound in Great Britain by Clays Ltd, Elcograf S.p.A.

The authorized representative in the EEA is Penguin Random House Ireland,
Morrison Chambers, 32 Nassau Street, Dublin D02 YH68

A CIP catalogue record for this book is available from the British Library

ISBN: 978-0-241-42131-4

www.greenpenguin.co.uk

Even our shadows are in love
when we walk.

Chantal Akerman,
My Mother Laughs (2019),

translated by
Daniella Shreir

I

GREECE, SEPTEMBER

I first saw her in a flea market in Athens buying two mechanical dancing horses. The man who sold them to her was slipping a battery into the belly of the brown horse, a super-heavy-duty zinc AA. He showed her that to start the horse, which was the length of two large hands, she had to lift up its tail. To stop it she must pull the tail down. The brown horse had a string tied to its neck and if she held the string upwards and outwards, she could direct its movements.

Up went the tail and the horse began to dance, its four hinged legs trotting in a circle. He then showed her the white horse, with its black mane and white hooves. Did she want him to slip an AA into its belly so it too could begin its dance? Yes, she replied in English, but her accent was from somewhere else.

I was watching her from a stall laid out with miniature plaster statues of Zeus, Athena, Poseidon, Apollo, Aphrodite. Some of these gods and goddesses had been turned into fridge magnets. Their final metamorphosis.

She was wearing a black felt trilby hat. I couldn't see much of her face because the blue clinical mask we were obliged to wear at this time was stretched over her mouth and nose. Standing with her was an elderly man, perhaps eighty years old. He did not respond to the horses with delight, as she was doing. Her body was animated, tall and lively as she pulled the strings upwards and outwards. Her companion was still, stooped and silent. I couldn't be sure, but it seemed as if the horses made him nervous. He watched them gloomily, even with foreboding. Perhaps he would persuade her to walk away and save her money.

When I glanced at the woman's feet, I noticed her scuffed brown leather shoes with high snakeskin heels. Her right toe lightly tapped, or perhaps danced, in time with the horses, who, guided by her hand, were now trotting together.

I hoped they could hear me calling to them under the Attica sky.

She paused to adjust her hat, tipping it forwards over her eyes.

As her fingers searched for a strand of hair tucked under her hat, she looked in my direction – not directly at me, but I sensed she knew I was there. It was eleven in the morning, but the mood she transmitted to me at that moment was dark and soft, like midnight. A light shower of rain began to fall on Athens, and with it came the smell of warm ancient stones and petrol from the cars and scooters.

She bought both of the horses, and when she walked off with them wrapped in newspaper, the old man, her companion, linked his arm with hers. They disappeared into the crowd. She seemed to be about my age, thirty-four, and like me she was wearing a tightly belted green rain-coat. It was almost identical to mine, except hers had three gold buttons sewn on to the cuffs. We obviously wanted the same things. My startling thought at that moment was that she and I were the same person. She was me and I was her. Per-haps she was a little more than I was. I sensed she had known I was standing nearby and that she was taunting me.

One, two, three.

I made my way to the stall and asked the man if I could see the horses. He told me that he had just sold the last two, but he had other mech-anical dancing animals, a selection of dogs, for example.

No, it was the horses I wanted. Yes, he said, but what people tend to like is how you lift up the tail of the animal to start the dance and push it down to stop. The tail is more interesting than a boring switch, he said, it's even like magic, and with this tail I could start or end the magic any time I liked. What did it matter if it was a dog and not a horse?

My piano teacher, Arthur Goldstein, had told me the piano was not the instrument, I was the instrument. He talked of my perfect pitch, my desire and ability to learn at the age of six, how all that he had taught me did not dissolve the next day. Apparently, I was a miracle. A miracle. A miracle. I had once heard him say to a journalist, No, Elsa M. Anderson is not in a trance when she plays, she is in flight.

The man asked if I wanted him to slip a super-heavy-duty zinc AAA battery into one of the dogs. He pointed to a creature that looked more like a fox, with an abundance of porcelain fur and a tail that curled over its back.

Yes, he said, the magic would start again, but this time with a curved tail. The dogs were smaller than the horses and could stand in the palm of my hand.

It seemed the horses were not the instrument,

it was the longing for magic and flight that was the instrument.

You are a beautiful lady. What do you do in life?

I told him I was a pianist.

Ah, so she was right, he said.

Who was right?

The lady who bought the horses. She told me you are famous.

When I tightened the belt of my raincoat so it cut into my waist, he made an exploding sound like a bomb.

You must drive your sweetheart mad, he said.

I reached into my pocket and took out the apple I had bought that morning from a grocery store. It was cool and taut like another skin. I held it against my burning cheek. And then I bit into it.

Look at this dog here, said the man who had sold her the horses. It's a spitz, the oldest breed in central Europe. She descends from the Stone Age. I looked at the porcelain white fur of the Stone Age spitz and shook my head. Sorry, lady, he laughed, the last two horses have found a home. My customer saw you looking at her. He lowered his voice and gestured to me to come closer.

She told me, That woman wants the horses, but I want the horses and I got here first.

I felt she had stolen something from me, something that I would miss in my life. I walked away from the stall of dancing animals, bereft, towards a wagon piled with pistachio nuts. Lying on the ground next to the wagon was the black felt trilby hat the woman had been wearing. She had tucked a small sprig of a delicate, pale pink flower into its grey ribbon. I had seen these same flowers on the slopes of the hills of the Acropolis on a walk earlier that morning. Perhaps they would have been growing there when real horses pulled carriages loaded with marble to build the Parthenon.

I picked the hat up and looked for her and the old man but couldn't see them anywhere. Her male companion was about the same age as my teacher, Arthur Goldstein.

At that moment I decided to keep the trilby hat. The horses were hers and not mine. It seemed like a fair exchange. I put it on right there in the market, tipping it forwards over my eyes, as she had done. Another thing. When she walked away with the horses, she had turned around briefly to look at a cat sleeping on a low wall near to where I was standing.

I had taken to making lists every day.

> <u>Pianos owned</u>
> Bösendorfer grand
> Steinway

I had stopped there and did not mention the more humble childhood piano.

After a while I checked my ferry ticket to the island of Poros and saw I had two hours to kill before I had to make my way to the port of Piraeus.

2

Max and Bella were sipping small cups of sweet Greek coffee on the rooftop of Café Avissinia, overlooking the Acropolis. They were both distinguished violinists. They thought that if it came to it, they might spend winter in Athens and buy warm jumpers. Bella would also look for a couple of jumpsuits, which were useful for playing cello, her second instrument. They admired my hat and asked me where I had bought it. I told them about the horses and the woman with the old man.

Doesn't sound like you tried very hard to return her hat. Why do you want the horses so much?

Max and Bella looked at me knowingly, but what did they know?

They knew I was a child prodigy and they knew how my foster-parents gifted me, age six, to Arthur Goldstein, who adopted me so I could become a resident pupil at his music school. I had been moved from a humble house near Ipswich in Suffolk to a grander house in Richmond, London. They knew about my audition and then scholarship to the Royal Academy of Music, they knew about the international prizes and Carnegie Hall, the recordings of recital work and piano concertos under the baton of the greatest conductors, most recently, and fatally, in the Golden Hall in Vienna. They knew about my acclaimed interpretations of Bach, Mozart, Chopin, Liszt, Ravel, Schumann, and they knew I had lost my nerve and was making mistakes. They knew I was now thirty-four. No lovers. No children. There was not a homely cup of coffee perched on my piano, teaspoon tucked into the saucer, a dog in the background, a river view outside my window or a companion making pancakes behind the scenes. And they knew about the concert I had messed up three weeks ago while playing Rachmaninov's Piano Concerto No. 2

and how I had walked off the stage in Vienna. I had played it many times before that particular concert. They knew I was heading for the Greek island of Poros to teach a thirteen-year-old boy. Just three piano lessons had been scheduled. We had agreed I would be paid by the hour in cash. Perhaps they thought I needed cheering up. Max and Bella announced they had a surprise for me. They had booked a trip on a boat with their friend Vass, a fisherman, who would take me diving for sea urchins before my first lesson.

Bella looked happy. Being in love with Max obviously made her think she could say anything she liked because she was wrapped in love. Look, Elsa, we know it's as much about Arthur as anything else. I mean what an arse he is, Arthur. We get it that you were his inspiration, his child muse, even his salvation, frankly. No one could live up to that. Elsa, he is a short man. With complexes.

She drew out the word *c-o-m-p-l-e-x-e-s*.

Who doesn't have a few of those?

Well, for a start he wears a nine-foot cravat in case no one notices him.

Yes, I said, that's one of the reasons why I love him.

Arthur had written to me after that fatal concert. *I felt you were not there when you walked on stage. Where were you, Elsa?*

Far away.

I had lost where we were under the baton of M. The orchestra went one way, the piano went another way. My fingers refused to bend for Rachmaninov and I began to play something else. Arthur had taught me at six years old to 'detach my mind from commonplace things', but it seemed that commonplace things had walked into my mind that night.

Max asked me if it was true that Arthur was now living in Sardinia. I told him it was true. He owned a small house in a town famous for its melons, sixty-four kilometres from Cagliari. He had been holidaying there for years, but now he had made it his home.

They wanted to know why.

He thinks love is more possible in the south.

Does Arthur have a lover?

I don't know.

They had meant it as a joke because he was now eighty. I never knew anything about his romantic life. I had not once seen Arthur with a partner, though I suspected he had his own arrangements. He was fifty-two when he adopted me, so maybe the most inflamed parts of his libido had been tamed.

Also, Bella said, as if she had made a list of mysteries to be solved and I was one of them, we don't know why you are teaching random children with no talent. You know, Elsa, every conservatoire in the world would employ you as an eminent professor. Get real.

I tried to get real in a way that would please Bella, so I said, Yes, I am teaching to pay the rent and buy a kebab until the pandemic settles. It wasn't true, my savings would tide me over, but I wanted to pull the tail down on everything I was feeling at this moment. Arthur was my teacher, but he was also a sort of father. The only father I had, and I loved him without measure. When I was young, he always sat by my side when I played. Your fingers are asleep, he'd shout, what is the point of teaching a sleeper? At the same time my fingers were lively. Trembling. I didn't know how to be to please him.

I had no desire to scare my own students.

Bella leaned across the table and kissed my cheek. We had known each other for a long time. Her ex-husband, Rajesh, had been a pupil at Arthur's summer school for a month. He and I had met when we were twelve, and had remained close friends ever since. In fact, I had introduced Bella to Rajesh when they were both twenty. They had married three years later, which no one at the time had understood. Now they had recently separated and she had hooked up with Max in Athens. I felt this long history, and her concern, in her kiss. To touch my cheek with her lips was quite a dangerous thing to do. I had lost track of where we were in the various waves of the virus. The big lockdowns were over, but everyone was still afraid.

Elsa, Bella said, please forget about the Rach and smile again.

Sergei Rachmaninov never smiled. His powerful left hand, his stern face, the sadness that lifted as he wrote Piano Concerto No. 2. Maybe he would smile at the way we always called him Rach, as if he were a friend dropping by to borrow a phone charger. I had listened to his big musical thoughts from the age of fifteen. For a while, Arthur and I had worked together on nothing but Rach and Tchaikovsky, because, as he had shown me, Rachmaninov was in love with Tchaikovsky, yet was much more structurally innovative. Although we lived in different centuries, both Rach and I were popular soloists at a young age, giving concerts at various conservatoires.

I gestured to the waiter, a small wave of my fingers, perhaps in the manner of a diva. Let's move on, I suggested to my friends, let me invite you to a glass of ouzo. I have to get to the port of Piraeus. The waiter did the honours and we raised our glasses not quite knowing what to say next. Someone had painted the words *Death Drugs Life Beauty* in black paint under an archway of city jasmine that seemed to be having a second autumn flowering.

I put on the hat and heard myself in communion with the woman who had bought the horses. I am going to find you, I said to her in my head. In exchange for your hat, you will give me the horses.

Bella turned her head away to disguise whatever expression she had just exchanged with Max.

I just don't get it, she said. That concert you walked out of. I mean, Rach had giant hands. He could span twelve piano keys from the tip of his little finger to the tip of his thumb.

Never bothered me before, I replied, but what I was thinking about were the pink acrylic nails worn by the model on the cover of the in-flight shopping magazine on my way to Athens. Her pale hand had looked like a corpse to me, every freckle and line airbrushed out. She held between her limp fingers the stem of a cocktail glass which was half full of a pink liquid to match her nails. Some sort of liqueur. Apparently, this drink made emotions. That's what it said, emotions were made with this liqueur. At the same time I was playing in my head a melancholy mazurka by Frédéric Chopin, Op. 17, No. 4. Bella tapped me on the shoulder. If you see Rajesh when you return to London, tell him he owes me six months of our mortgage.

Now it was Max's turn. Hey, Elsa, I don't know what happened, but everyone wants you to play again. It's like you've cancelled yourself. I adjusted the hat, tipping it forwards. A chorus of birds started to sing me out of the building when I began to walk down the steps of the rooftop to the exit.

Bella was calling out to me. I had left my phone on the table. The ringtone was Birdsong. As I walked back to get it, a species of bird trilled and warbled. It sang every time I received a text message. Arthur in Sardinia was asking me on WhatsApp to visit him. My fingers tapped the words: *But I work.*

Be careful of your hands, he texted back.

I suppose that, like the liqueur in the magazine, my hands made emotions. And then he wrote in capital letters with his ancient right hand, the hand that would grab my wrist as a child and lift it off the keys when he wanted me to use the pedals.

WHAT ABOUT THE BLUE?

A week before the Rachmaninov concert I had decided to dye my hair blue. Arthur tried to dissuade me. After all, my long brown hair, always plaited and coiled around my head, was my signature look. Elsa M. Anderson, the piano virtuoso who in some ways resembled a prima ballerina. In my teens I experimented with two plaited bunches, pinning them into spheres on either side of my head. Arthur thought this style lacked gravitas, but I kept it for a while. My dear, he said, if you are hell-bent on wrecking your lovely hair, you must go to my own salon in Kensington.

Blue was a separation from my DNA. We both knew that I wanted to sever the possibility that I resembled my unknown parents. Arthur was bewildered that I had no desire to search for them. Or to make contact with my foster-parents. From the age of ten he had told me I could look at 'the documents' any time I liked.

He meant the adoption papers. I think he was forever preparing himself for the inevitable search I would begin to find my birth parents. But I never wanted to read 'the documents' and told him so. Arthur always replied, I admire your great strength.

By the time he arrived at the salon, I had already been there for three hours. The colourist had to bleach my hair before applying the dye. Arthur had bought us both a sandwich from Pret. He handed me mine and confided that he had also purchased two chocolate marshmallow biscuits which were melting in his pocket. For some reason he wanted to discuss Nietzsche's relationship with Wagner, not just with me, but with all the staff at the salon. Perhaps he was nervous about the blue. The stylist who was working on my hair in tandem with the colourist asked him who these men were.

Nietzsche was the all-too-human philosopher, Arthur said, Wagner the composer, mostly of inflamed operas. Out of the two of them, Nietzsche was more likely to have dyed his tash blue. So what was their relationship? It's a matter of temperature, Arthur replied, *scalding* would be the word for their relationship. It seemed that to get away from his crush on Wagner, Nietzsche began listening to the French composer Bizet, because it was music that had the morning sun in it. Yes, said Arthur, Nietzsche decided Bizet's music had 'a more sunburned outlook'. Arthur sat down and started to unwrap his sandwich. As it happens, he said, Nietzsche's own compositions were rather ecclesiastical for someone who was screaming 'God is dead' from every mountain and bridge. He played piano and composed until quite late in life, but he felt he had failed as a composer, which was probably true. Wagner thought so too. Frankly, whatever was going on in Nietzsche's head was better expressed in philosophy and not in music. My hair was being painted with a small brush. The smell of bleach made my eyes water. Well, you don't know that, I said, as the colourist pushed my chin down, you don't know anything about Nietzsche's own compositions, the ones he never wrote.

Ah, but I do, Arthur replied mysteriously, some of us are creators – he bit into his egg mayonnaise sandwich – and the rest of us are performers.

Perhaps he was talking about my own early attempts at composition. It was as if he knew I could hear something that he did not understand, and resented it. As my fingers found the keys, I discovered that I had a point of view. All I had to do to tear it open was listen.

The stylist asked me to shift in my seat so she could retie the back of my protective black gown.

Nietzsche rightly believed, Arthur continued, dabbing at his lips with a napkin, that music was the highest art, the essence of being. Yet he broke with Wagner's infinitely exhausting melodies just as one breaks a plate and sees no point in putting it together again. Arthur was now forensically removing the egg white from his egg mayonnaise sandwich. The idea of a more sunburned outlook seemed to thrill him, probably because of his house in Sardinia. I agree with Nietzsche, he said, tossing his walking stick on the floor, that love is more possible in the south.

Blue has to sit on a very light blonde. The whole process took nearly six hours. I could tell Arthur was excited, appalled and a little agitated. We sipped tea, I with my hair wrapped in foils. At one point he kissed my hand as if I was about to have major surgery. He wouldn't stop talking. Had he told them, he asked, about collecting me from school and how one day his long, white chiffon scarf nearly got caught in the wheels of the car and strangled him, Isadora Duncan style? Elsa is *en-trance-d* by Isadora, he whispered to the colourist, who was now giving the intern instructions on where to buy her a quinoa salad. Arthur knew I was reading the autobiography of Isadora Duncan, the mother of modern dance, as she was sometimes described. I often watched the students of Isadora's technique on YouTube as they performed her choreographies, mostly accompanied by the music of Bach, Mendelssohn, Chopin, Schumann. They were barefoot and wore flimsy togas. I think the idea was to show me how to be happy and free.

My colourist was still in conversation with

the intern. She added a Coke to the lunch list and explained how it had to be as cold as a corpse.

A corpse is not necessarily cold, my dear, Arthur interrupted. It takes at least twelve hours for blood to cool in the human body.

It seemed that Arthur was going to stay until the end, so she suggested he have a wash and blow-dry himself. The director of the salon, Rafael from Rotherhithe and Rio, as he described himself, was used to being discreet about the effort it took to raise the chair to get Arthur's head to reach the basin. The youngest intern suddenly arrived with three cushions. At last his head was in the basin. Everyone wanted him to drown.

When the time came for the blue dye to be rinsed, Arthur was somewhat breathless. He knew I would be playing the Golden Hall in Vienna with blue hair in a week's time. The audience who had come to listen to their favourite piano virtuoso might wonder if she'd been replaced by someone else.

The colourist was very tense.

For a moment I thought about my birth mother.

And then my foster-mother.

My new sleek blue hair rippled down my back to just above my waist.

I had two mothers. One had given me up. And I had given up the woman who had replaced her. I could hear them gasping.

Arthur flung his arms in the air. My dear, he said, as I don't have an open sleigh to be pulled by huskies across the stormy streets of London, we will share a taxi. You, Elsa M. Anderson, are now a natural blue.

3

I made my way to Gate E8 in Piraeus Port to board the boat from Athens to the Greek island of Poros. Everyone had to wear masks on public transport. It was a rough crossing. The staff walked around distributing sick bags to those who raised their hands to signal they felt nauseous behind their masks. The autumn sun lit the Aegean waves as the wind lifted them. Now that the pandemic had blown into the third decade of the twenty-first century, there were laminated notices on the walls of the boat telling passengers to keep 1.5 metres apart. The safety card tucked into the pocket of my chair promised that every life jacket was equipped with a whistle. There were two screens side by side on the wall, one advertising a brand of heater, the other a type of ice cream. A couple sat in the aisle seats opposite me wearing transparent plastic visors under which they wore not one but two clinical masks. They were sipping iced coffee through straws and they had pierced their masks to get the straws into their mouths. While the boat rocked on the sunlit waves, Rajesh sent me a text about earthquakes in Greece. He had spent his time looking up the Richter scale of the quake that had recently caused damage in Greece and Turkey. I called him to ask how he was doing in London. He told me that if he were to carry a whistle in his jacket pocket to blow every time he felt anxious, it would never leave his lips. I thought it best not to mention Bella's request that he pay his share of the mortgage. For the rest of the journey I put on headphones and listened to the violin concerto that Philip Glass had dedicated to his father. I could hear my heart beating as I gazed at the dazzling waves.

4

I had arranged to meet my student and his father outside a hotel on the port. I made my way to this hotel, which seemed closed, so I sat on the deserted steps to the entrance. I could still taste ouzo on my lips.

The afternoon sun fell gently on the blue clock tower built high on the hill amongst olive and cypress trees. The violins of the mourning concerto and the rhythm of the boat had not yet left my body. After a while, someone shouted, There she is. It was Marcus, who I had only met on Zoom. He was tugging at his father's arm, pulling him towards me. Marcus wore a knee-length T-shirt and flip-flops with big white plastic daisies on the toes. When I waved, his father shouted, Chill out, little man. Marcus was thirteen. They walked towards me through the sunshine and screeching gulls.

My student's father reached out to shake my hand. He wore a suit and an expensive brand of trainers.

Please call me Steve.

His hair was scraped back into a ratty pony-tail. He was something in shipping, originally from Baltimore, and rich, but he looked like he had once been a hippy and believed in peace and promiscuity. Apparently, there was a problem with his car. It had been stopping and starting on the way to the port. Steve thought I would be better off getting a taxi to the cottage they had rented for me. The housekeeper would be at the property and she would show me how everything worked. He wanted to know my plans for the weekend. I told him I was diving for sea urchins on Sunday.

Whose boat?

He's called Vass, I said.

Steve grinned. Yeah, Vass's fishing methods are quite basic.

He called out to someone and before I knew it a taxi had arrived.

You are famous, Madame Blue, he said to me, we are keen to make everything as smooth as possible. He took out a little black book from his jacket pocket and asked for my autograph, pushing a heavy silver fountain pen into my hand. I signed his book, *Elsa M. Anderson*. Don't forget to take off your hat when you dive for urchins, he quipped.

I'll see you on Monday, Marcus, I said. Wind chimes jingled on the fishing boats. Gulls swooped above the nets piled on deck.

Speak, little man. His father poked his arm.

Marcus lifted his right hand and wiggled his fingers at me. Then he bent down and adjusted the white daisy on his flip-flop.

So, Marcus, we'll be finding a mechanic to figure out what's going on with our car, right?

Steve upped the volume of his voice. As if speaking loudly would somehow wither the flamboyant plastic daisy on his child's shoe.

*

The world was spinning slowly backwards to a memory of Arthur picking me up from school, a light coating of mascara on his eyelashes. He was talking about Chopin's nocturnes in B flat minor and E flat to a father in the playground. This father had made his way to school on his child's skateboard. While the man adjusted one of its wheels, Arthur explained to him that nocturnes were short piano works inspired by moods and feelings at night. The father interrupted him to loudly ask if he happened to have a spanner in his pocket.

The housekeeper was waiting for me at the cottage. She wore a mask and I searched my jacket pocket for mine. The tavernas all had a bottle of hand sanitizer on the table, not good for my hands, made from at least seventy per cent alcohol. I had read about a couple of drunks who had broken into the dispensers in a hospital in London to drink it. My agent had told me that soap and water was a more effective way to get rid of germs than sanitizer, as if he'd had a medical training. My hands were insured in America for millions of dollars. I had to take care of my hands. The basics were massaging them, drumming my fingers for circulation, soaking them first in warm water, then in cold, keeping my nails short, no varnish, no rings, moisturizing, stretching, no splinters or cuts, trying to sleep without lying on my arm.

Now that we were both masked and could not easily read the expressions on each other's faces, we had to use the translation app on our phones to understand each other. Greek to English, English to Greek. We gave up after a while. She showed me the fuse box with the switches for hot water, the cooker, lights in various rooms, but they were all labelled in Greek. I would have to look up on my app which switch was for hot water in the kitchen and which for the bathroom. The man who sold the horses was right. These switches performed the same function as turning the horses off and on, yet they did not elicit the same emotion. After all, the boiler did not start to dance when I flicked the switch up. And yet, in reality, the mechanism was the same. Up for on, down for off.

*

In the small garden at the back of the cottage three toads had come out to greet the sudden downpour of rain. White butterflies settled on the pale orange flowers planted around a fig tree. The air was warm and fragrant. That first day in Poros, I felt that the woman who had bought the horses was very close to me.

Maybe I am, I said to her.

Maybe you are what?

Famous.

And in flight, she said. In flight from your talent and from men.

I knew these were my own thoughts, but they made me a little sad.

Not a little, a lot, she said.

I decided to think of the woman who had bought the horses as my double. I heard her voice as music, a mood, or sometimes as a combination of two chords. She frightened me. She was more knowing than I was. She made me feel less alone.

For some reason my laptop would not let me change UK time to Greek time, so I had to keep adding two hours to British time. If it was five in the afternoon in London, it was seven in the evening in Poros. This bending of time, backwards and forwards, added to the unreality of being in Greece after the long lockdown. Meanwhile there were spiderwebs in the corners of every room in the cottage. When I opened the windows, the wind tossed them about. These webs had long been discarded by their makers, as I had been too.

I was a natural blue.
I am a natural blue.
I was, I am.

I was now and again trying something out in my mind, an embryonic symphony, a mental impression of harmonic combinations. These were the notes that had entered me the night I played in Vienna.

I was unwrapping the SARS-CoV-2 Rapid Antigen Test I was about to take here in Poros. The test kit was made in Hangzhou, China. This device, I suppose, was human history.

You are ducking and diving with your own history, she said.

I was ducking and diving with my own history. Up to the age of five, my foster-parents referred to me as Ann. They owned a piano, a Wurlitzer upright, that was the main thing, and they paid for piano lessons. A woman came to the house on Saturdays, then Wednesdays and Fridays. What with three lessons a week and all the practising, I was lost to the piano, they barely had a child. Certainly not a light-hearted child. They were kind people. Sometimes they asked me a question: Are you happy, Ann? I made sure I never looked into their pleading eyes. Then the Wurlitzer disappeared. When Arthur adopted me, I became Elsa. Much later, when I started to earn, I asked Arthur to send money to these foster-parents to pay them back for the lessons. He said he thought it was unnecessary. Unless I wanted to contact them, he thought it best to let this go. He was always very direct with me on this matter. No, he said, I don't want you to think you have to pay for your talent and capabilities, nor, and he actually tapped my nose, should you have to pay for being born and looked after reasonably well. I was looked after more than reasonably well. They offered me their love but I couldn't feel it.

Something was happening to my eyes. I wanted to cry but I couldn't make tears. Crying sounds came from my lips, but the tears, wet tears, were not there. Arthur had told me that now I had messed up the Rach at a major concert, the only venue that would have me was London St Pancras station. Passengers would drop coins into a paper cup while I played on one of the out-of-tune pianos in the shopping strip.

And what happened that night in Vienna?

I lost where we were under the baton of M. My fingers refused to work through the heavy natural-minor chord progressions that feature throughout. Neither could I work with the lighter, more delicate harmonies. The structure of Rach's mighty composition had unravelled. When I had watched the man in Athens slip the AA batteries into the bellies of the horses, I realized the letters *AA* were the initials of my birth name, Ann Anderson.

Maybe you are, she said.

Maybe I am what?

Looking for signs.

What sort of signs?

Reasons to live.

It was not a whisper.

I heard it as a chorus, perhaps even a title.

Later that night I nearly stepped on a large insect lying on the stone floor of my bedroom. Ants were crawling over and around it.

I thought it was a caterpillar. And then I saw its pincers and reckoned it was a scorpion. I found an egg flipper in the kitchen drawer, scooped up the scorpion and dropped it into the garden from the balcony. It reminded me of the creature woven into a kilim rug that Arthur kept in the music room in Richmond. I had often stared at it while practising Chopin's elating *Fantaisie-Impromptu*, Op. 66.

I checked the weather on my out-of-time laptop. There would be a wind of up to eighteen miles per hour for the expedition with Vass tomorrow.

Apparently, we would be joined by Tomas, who was a friend of Max's, a documentary film-maker from Berlin. I was looking forward to the boat trip. It was definitely a reason to live. When I was twelve, Arthur took me for the summer holiday to a house he had rented in Devon on the banks of the River Dart. In the mornings we worked on Bach's Prelude and Fugue No. 2 in C minor before I was freed for the afternoon. Arthur revealed Bach to me. His task, he said, was to awaken everything that was asleep inside me. And then I could escape.

There was a boat tied to the jetty. I taught myself to use the oars and then let the current take me away. I lay on my back and watched the birds in the reeds and the shifting clouds. Alone at last. My body was tall and lean. It seemed I was growing breasts. I took off my T-shirt and looked at them. They were private and they were mine. I was also growing hair. Down there. I slipped my fingers down my shorts and felt it, soft and silky. The English sun fell on my stomach and new breasts. Water lapped against the sides of the boat.

By the time I rowed back to the jetty there was music in my head, a phrase that came back six times. I suppose it was a kind of diary but it was not written in words. Birds, the splash of the oars, questions about sex, no mother, no father, a tangle of blackberries ripening in a field near my childhood house. I had made a pact with God. If I picked a berry near this field, I would die. It would reveal something to me that would do me in. I was in such a hurry that I scratched my arms on the hedgerows as I made my way back to the holiday house. I knew that somewhere in the house, Arthur was listening, and he was disapproving. After all, it would take a lifetime to learn how to play Bach.

5

Vass decided to sail after all. He said the wind would calm down. The boat was tipping upwards for about twenty minutes after we left the port. Max's friend Tomas, who was on the boat with us for the day, was feeling seasick. He was about thirty and wore round tortoise-shell spectacles. Vass told him to keep his eyes on the horizon, that would settle his stomach. We both looked out at the horizon. There had been a forest fire somewhere on the mainland, whipped up by the wind. A thick band of smoke floated across the sky. Its acrid smell was in the air, too. Tomas was promptly sick over his new Greek leather sandals. His spectacles had fallen off and now lay in a pool of vomit. Vass suggested he lie down on the bed on the lower deck. Now and again I was instructed to give 'the patient' water. I picked up his spectacles and Vass showed me how to switch on the little shower on deck to clean them. Tomas was lying flat out on his back. He was wearing shorts and a white T-shirt, now splattered with vomit. When I gave him his spectacles, I noticed his eyes were grey-blue, perhaps the colour of smoke. His hair was mousy and came down to his shoulders. Sunburn on his knees, mosquito bites on his shins.

He had bought a box of pastries for us all, he told me, the box was in his bag, please to help myself, almond cakes, a speciality from this region. I reached into his bag. He had packed a water bottle, a tube of sunblock, six cans of beer and a book about the French film director Agnès Varda. The little cake box was tied with a green ribbon. Before he was sick again, he told me I was kind.

Maybe I am.

When the wind had calmed and we pulled into a sheltered bay, Vass dived into the ocean, flipping downwards, head first. He held a fork in his right hand, an ordinary dinner-table fork, and a blue plastic carrier bag in his left hand. He could hold his breath underwater for three minutes while he plunged the fork into the urchin, turning it to the left and to the right, wrenching it off the rock. He told me to do the same and together we would slay enough urchins for a feast at sunset. I could also hold my breath for a long time under the deep Aegean, but I needed to surface more often than Vass. As I plunged my fork into the urchin and wiggled it about before the wrench, I tried to protect my fingers from the spines. The sun burst through the water and I was swimming in light.

The long lockdown during the pandemic had improved the clarity of the sea. There were many urchins on the rocks. My fork reached for one of them, my blue hair plaited and pinned up, arms stretching outwards and upwards. I discovered I was brutal. There were now about seven urchins in my blue bag. When I surfaced to take a breath, I could see Vass still underwater, working with his fork. I swam back to the boat, three spines in my fingers.

Tomas had recovered. He was showering naked on the deck and he was singing. I kept out of his way while he dressed, which involved washing the vomit out of his shorts and putting them on soaking wet. He walked over to me, holding two cans of beer and the box of almond cakes.

You're a killing machine in a bikini, he said.

We looked out at the smoke moving across the sky as we sipped beer. What came to me, transmitted through the smell of the forest fire on the mainland, was something to do with the burning of straw on the surrounding farms next to my first home in Suffolk. The farmers used to burn the leftover hay to make space for their winter seed beds, but when I was five, a wind was up and there had been a big fire. It had rampaged into the surrounding villages. The woman who taught me piano told us her lettuces had been ruined. The windows of my childhood house had been open and there was a layer of ash on the top of my piano. The Wurlitzer upright. The ash had blown inside the guts of the piano, too. There was talk of finding the child prodigy a new instrument. The day I came downstairs to find the Wurlitzer had disappeared was a wrench. Like the urchin violently being removed from its rock. I had clung to that piano, and now there was an absence in the space where it once stood. A surge of panic entered my body. I reached for an almond cake, sweet and moist, like marzipan, as if it were medication that might dull a pain resurfacing in the present.

By the time Vass swam back to the boat, Tomas and I were drunk. We had opened four of the beers and Tomas was singing a Joni Mitchell song to me. 'Big Yellow Taxi'. It was too high for him but he was enjoying the challenge of finding a voice within himself that was totally alien to his own deep voice. Vass got into the spirit of it all and sang the chorus with us as he opened the urchin.

The insides of the creatures were slimy, salty and intense. Tomas was still queasy. He explained he could not eat them, but he would help take their spines out of my fingers.

Vass had given me a bowl of hot water and told me to plunge my fingers into it. I asked Tomas what sort of films he made. Mostly documentaries, he replied. He liked Agnès Varda because she had once said she made documentaries to remind herself of reality. Here I was in this reality, living the life on Vass's boat while Tomas removed the spines from my insured fingers with tweezers. My right hand was resting on his lap and I felt his erection. It was exciting, the spines being pulled from my fingers and his desire.

6

In the first five minutes of our lesson, Marcus told me their favoured pronoun. They were not sure the piano was their instrument. They preferred cello but mostly preferred their puppy above any instrument. I was introduced to Skippy with more enthusiasm than anything else. Skippy was a sentimental name for such a fierce dog, a German shepherd, fifteen months old, black and brown and in love with Marcus. The first thing Skippy did was to try and eat my hat. Her hat. Why do you always wear that trilby, Marcus wanted to know.

I stole it, I replied. My young student gazed at me with new respect.

At one point we heard something smash. It's

Skippy trashing the place, Marcus said. Are you sensitive to noise?

I told them how Mozart's ear was so delicate the sound of a trumpet too close made him faint. Marcus fell about laughing.

I thought they were talented despite their reluctance to work with the piano. I sensed that for Marcus it was not the instrument that could speak on behalf of them.

I suggested we work with cello, their second instrument. Marcus played for me the Sarabande from Bach's Cello Suite No. 1.

But you are holding your breath, I said.

Most of the lesson was a conversation. I asked Marcus if they thought a relationship with our instrument was as complicated as any other relationship in life?

After a while, cello and child began to breathe together. All the same, Marcus would have to proceed with piano because that's why I was here. I sat on a chair next to them while they played. When I wanted to correct a mistake, I lifted their wrist off the keys. You are stealing my hand, Marcus said, like you stole the hat.

I made a decision to never do that again.

Their Norwegian mother seemed proud of her exuberant and charming child. When I left she said, We know about the concert in Vienna, everyone does, but as far as I am concerned, I feel lucky to have you here. She put ninety euro on the table and pretended to scroll down her phone while I picked up the notes and stuffed them into my purse.

I like to listen to him play cello, she said. It warms up the house.

It seemed that Marcus had not shared their pronoun of choice with family. She told me some of her memories of her home country, how shrimps are tasty in January when the water is cold, also the succulent crayfish she used to buy from a boat in Oslo harbour.

Hei! she yelled to her child.

Hei! Marcus yelled back.

She wore apricot-coloured lipstick, her blonde hair pinned up in a high bun, Brigitte Bardot style.

The small diamonds in her ears, the size of pin-heads, glistened on her lobes like tiny tears.

I invited Marcus to join me for ice cream at a local café. I felt at ease in their company. Marcus said they'd prefer lemonade and gulped it down in three seconds. The kids in the village were always asking them to join the local orchestra. Why not? You like playing with other musicians, right? They admitted it was true, but there were problems. What sort of problems? Marcus plucked at the daisy on their right flip-flop and somehow managed to pull it off. The rest of our rendezvous was about figuring how to stick it back on to the criss-cross by the toe. While we did this, Marcus told me where to buy Greek slippers. They were originally made from leather, they said, with fifty nails pierced into the sole. Each slipper had a large woollen pompom on the toe. Apparently, in the Greek Revolution, the pompom was a hiding place for sharp objects, like, Marcus giggled, you could whip out a dagger hidden in your pompom.

They asked why I stole the hat. I told them

about the woman who had got to the horses before I did. Marcus thought it was a crazy situation. They wanted to know about Arthur Goldstein.

I think he's disappointed in me, I said.

Yeah, Marcus said. My dad's disappointed in me too. I am supposed to be his little me but I'll leave that to my older brother.

Where was their brother?

Boarding school in England.

They were sucking at the straw. The glass was empty and it made a hissing sound. The wind lifted the white napkins on our table into the air, floating for a while above our heads.

Marcus reached out to touch my hair.

I'm a natural blue, I said. I've brought three aerosols of dye with me. By the way, I want you to practise Brahms's Piano Sonata No. 1 in C minor, Op. 49.

Even for an exceptionally gifted student like Marcus this was an impossible task.

I've seen photos of Arthur Goldstein. Marcus pretended he hadn't heard me. He's about the same size as Skippy. And he's gay.

Yes, I said, there was not a day he lived without the threat of violence and ridicule, especially when he was younger. He was born in 1941 after all. It was not easy for him to adopt me, but it helped that he was internationally respected as a teacher. I told Marcus how he said to me, age six, If I am to teach you, I will take you very far from your life as you know it.

I wish you would take me far away from my parents, Marcus said. Why don't you start up a school?

I explained that I went to a proper school as well. There were no resident pupils at Arthur's school, except for me. Just classes and concerts and summer schools. Arthur wanted us to learn to play together, to be less haphazard. When I was sixteen, I had a crush on the director of a conservatoire in Estonia who attended the summer school to hear us play. He was my age now, thirty-four, handsome, charismatic. He thought Arthur had neglected aspects of my technique and I was dazed with longing and lust. Playing a duet with him I nearly fainted, his elbows and fingers so close to mine, but when

Arthur sensed this he went crazy and told him to pack his bags and return to Estonia. When I asked him why, Arthur said, What do you mean, why? Because I am in love with him and he's favoured my best student. Marcus laughed.

Maybe the man from Estonia liked taller men?

In the meanwhile, I said, you can also practise Ligeti's exciting Sonata for Solo Cello.

Anything to get away from Dad working at home, Marcus said.

It seemed to me their father had already written his child's composition. This infuriated me for my own reasons. I had spent a whole lesson encouraging his child not to hold their breath, so I asked Marcus how they relaxed.

I like to dance with Skippy to Prince.

I like to watch Isadora Duncan dance on YouTube.

Who's she?

The mother of modern dance.

How modern?

She was born in 1877.

7

I was starting up a friendship with Tomas, who had been sick on the boat. He was moving to Paris in the next few weeks to write his documentary on Agnès Varda. We hired mopeds and drove around the island. He was a cautious driver and I often overtook him, beeping loudly as I passed his scooter. Every taxi driver on the road overtook him too, and so did a seventy-five-year-old man on a bicycle.

He wanted to know more about my life as a concert pianist.

I realized I was holding my breath.

Perhaps my life had shattered to such a degree there was no point in putting it together again for Tomas.

*

Alone with the spiderwebs in the cottage in Poros, I made a salad of watermelon and feta cheese. At times I heard the midnight resonance of the woman who had bought the horses. I listened to her tone, writing it down, making a score of sorts as the sun slipped slowly into the glowing sea. Isadora Duncan was also in my thoughts, as usual. Above all else, she believed in what she called freedom of expression: 'I will show you just how beautiful the human dancing body can be when it is inspired by thoughts.' Presumably she meant the thoughts that moved her upwards and outwards.

There are thoughts that move me inwards and downwards.

It is so abject to express this loneliness within me. I am not sure I can take the freedom to find a language in music to reveal it. I have, after all, learned to conceal it. The old masters are my shield. Beethoven. Bach. Rachmaninov. Schumann. Their inner lives are valuable without measure.

You are speaking in the present tense, she says.

I glimpse myself in the mirror wearing her hat.

Maybe I am.

Maybe you are what?

Looking for reasons to live.

There was still one urchin spine in my finger as I listened to world news on my laptop. The salty feta. The sweet juicy melon. The butterflies settling on the loquat tree in the garden. The robotic voice of the presenter reading the news. Cicadas. Figs falling from the trees. Laughter in the garden below.

I should never have tuned into the news.

Deep within me, deep, deep, without an anchor, this rage at those who had made the content of the news. The same old language. The same composition. Repeated over and over. In time there would be a statue to honour them in every city in the world. Alongside their bronze doubles, the slavers and captains of empire.

Maybe I am.
   Maybe you are what?
   Crushed.

That evening as I continued to write, I cancelled my sadder thoughts. It didn't make them go away, but I was still in love with Isadora's bare feet and arms. It was a way to be in the world. Upwards and outwards.

8

The next lesson with Marcus was turbulent. They seemed to have rowed with their father and had obviously been crying. I suggested they play cello and I improvise on the piano. We did this for a while.

I was struck by the poise of Marcus as they played, their grace and attention. I was wrong to think they took nothing seriously. In the break we looked at the Isadora films on my phone. We could hear their parents arguing upstairs. Steve was working from home and this was a problem for his child and wife. He was a big presence. We could try and dance like her, I suggested.

You do the dancing, Marcus said, I'll take over the piano. What shall I play?

We found the music for a Schubert sonata

and Marcus took my place on the piano stool. I unlaced my new white leather Greek sandals and loosened my plait. It was awkward, ridiculous, to attempt to imitate such a peculiar, archaic language. A style of dancing that was close to ballet, yet had crashed through most of its conventions. After a while, I decided it was more interesting to respect it than mock it.

To lift up my right arm and then my left hand and transmit a response to the humiliation of the Golden Hall in Vienna brought me closer to the thoughts I had cancelled than I wanted to be. Marcus aligned the music with my dance as they felt it, so that in the end they were improvising with Schubert but creating something else. I realized Marcus had a profound musical intelligence. After a while they suggested we change places. How about I play Schubert and they would do the Isadora?

It was all leaping and running and falling with Marcus, arms stretched upwards to the gods, pleading, beseeching, escaping their wrath and thunder. Schubert was not the right mood, so I played something else. The door to the practice room suddenly crashed open. Someone had kicked it from the other side. Marcus's father walked in, carrying a plate of spaghetti bolognese. He was trying to work on his computer in the basement, he said, but there was all this thudding coming from the practice room. Now he wanted to eat his lunch and the noise was even worse. He asked me in front of his child if I was a dance teacher or a music teacher? For what was he paying me? If I was a dance teacher, the rate was lower than that of a world-famous piano virtuoso teaching his son.

A musician needs to feel Schubert in their body in order to play with sensitivity, I replied.

Marcus was frozen, kneeling on the floor, their arms and head lifted towards the ceiling.

Stand up, little man, their father instructed them.

Marcus refused to stand up.

Steve walked over to his child. Again, he asked Marcus to stand up. He was in a rage. Cold rage. Marcus stared at the wall and did not move. They were kneeling on their left knee, right leg extended, toes balletically pointing outwards.

Steve's eyes flicked towards the window as if he suddenly feared we were being observed by a casual passer-by. Outside, the sea was calm. Two cypress trees reached for the sky. He told me I was fired and left the room.

I suggested we take Skippy for a walk to the port. We ran down the steps towards the sea. It seemed to me the day had been full of beauty and violence and tragedy.

You know what, Marcus, have a break from the piano and take up your cello. I have a friend in Athens who is a cellist. Her name is Bella, she will teach you cello better than I can.

Marcus picked up a small pine cone lying on the path and slipped it into their pocket.

You can play duets together. Cello is her second instrument. Your homework from me is to compose something of your own that lasts two minutes, twelve seconds. That's hard to do, but it's the only rule.

Well, Marcus said, I never know what I'm doing on the cello.

I told them that Isadora was certain that if

she could tell you all about what it meant, there would be no point in dancing it.

The laces of my sandals had come undone. Marcus and the hound had to wait while I sat on a bench to criss-cross the white leather straps up my shins. A knot on the left, again on the right. The dog's wet pink tongue hanging out of his mouth, his eyes staring at Marcus with devotion. When you go back to London, Marcus said, emboldened by the love of Skippy and the fact that I did not seem at all put out by being sacked, please stop wearing that trilby. Why not buy yourself a woollen hat with a bobble?

9

Tomas and I decided to drink a lot of alcohol together at our favourite bar. We perched on a wobbly wooden bench, our knees touching, a poster of Salvador Dalí pinned on the wall opposite us.

So, he said, peering at me through his tortoiseshell spectacles, now you've been fired and have to leave your nice cottage, let's talk about your driving.

What about my driving?

Clearly, he said, you are a reckless driver and do not value your life.

Clearly, I replied, you have too much fear of losing your life.

Ah, he sighed, then we are a perfect mix, you need more fear and I need less.

We ordered another round of margaritas.

He was curious about the dresses I wore for my concerts. Where were they? The dresses were hanging in my wardrobe in London. It was as if they belonged to someone who had died. Always sleeveless. Sometimes backless. Mostly cut from fluid fabrics that packed well for travelling. I asked him what he wore to write his documentary film scripts.

Here in Greece he wore shorts and sometimes a sarong. In Berlin it was more like jeans and jumpers. In Paris he wore lighter trousers, maybe even a suit if he had a meeting with executives. He pointed out that I was taller than him. He wondered if my parents were tall as well.

No, I replied, my father is practically a midget.

I was referring to Arthur. There was no way I wanted to go into the adoption story.

Tomas started to sing 'Moonage Daydream' to his margarita.

I did know that my biological father was not named in the documents. Arthur had told me he was not significant, that this man had not wished to acknowledge my birth. Perhaps he was tall. Perhaps my birth mother was tall. Perhaps I was conceived on a dead donkey with rotting eye sockets. What did I know?

I'd like to get to know you better, Tomas said.

As it was my last night in Poros, we set off to swim at a beach called Love Bay at two in the morning. The bay was surrounded by a pine forest, the azure water still and flat like a lake.

Take it, take it, I heard my double say.

Take what?

I undressed and left my clothes on the sand. I was not at ease with my body, not even in the darkness of night. It had been unloved, perhaps for ever. Untouched by a lover for a long time. I didn't know what to do with it when it was not in conversation with a piano. Or how to respond to the way Tomas gazed at the green jewel pierced through my belly button.

We waded into the cool flat water, and when we dived under, I continued the conversation with the woman who had bought the horses. My horses.

Yes, she said, you have pulled the tail up. Take it.

I swam over to Tomas. We moved in closer. I put my arms around his neck and my lips were on his lips. He was shivering though it was a warm night. His desire was stronger than my own. Suddenly his hands were all over me and his fingers inside me.

It was not what I wanted.

Yes, she said, but what tempest is bigger than two humans naked and kissing? You pulled up the tail and considered it, but you do not wish to make love on Love Bay. That is acceptable. Maybe the kiss is a rehearsal for someone else, like a concert?

I pulled away from Tomas and swam towards the pine trees. He caught up with me and tried to kiss me again.

No, I said to him, I don't want to make love on Love Bay.

He looked disappointed and hurt, but I reckoned it was not the worst thing that had happened to him in his life. What do you do if there is not equal desire? Or at least enough desire?

You pull away, my double said. Desire is never fair.

Tomas swam alone for a while. And then he caught up with me.

I've changed my mind, he said. You are not kind.

We flipped on to our backs and breathed in the smell of the pines.

Why would I have sex with you to be kind?

He laughed and I laughed, but we didn't mean it and then we flipped underwater so we didn't have to speak.

10

I was sorry to leave Greece. I knew I was running away from everything, but I did not want to plunge a fork into my life and look at it too closely. Marcus saw me off at the port. Their father, who was so keen to police his child's body with his *little man* provocations, was alone drinking a bottle of whisky on the beach. I had told Vass about what had happened. He offered Marcus a job cleaning his boat on Saturdays so they could get away from Steve from Baltimore. Apparently, he'd been spotted sitting at various tavernas barking out orders, but no one had ears for him, not even to serve him a glass of water. All the same I was anxious he would make his child cry again. Marcus's mother had agreed to three lessons with Bella. When I rang my old friend to tell her I'd been sacked and to confirm she had a small job, Bella told me she was pleased to be spending the days having endless sex with Max. Being unemployed was not so bad. At the moment she could afford bread, a few olives and tomatoes and as much cheap wine as she could bear. Frankly she and Max only got up at six in the evening, but okay, she would take the job, thanks, and how did I get on with Tomas?

It was the last few days of September. The sea was still warm but it was now colder in the evenings. I was glad to wear my hat. Her hat.

I had tucked a sprig of jasmine inside the ribbon. So now in my head, under the hat, I heard the low-level buzzing of the bees that had been at work inside the jasmine bush. Like a drone or something about to explode.

I I

LONDON, OCTOBER

I was in North London when I next saw the woman who had bought the horses. I thought she seemed ambivalent about looking in my direction. I was sitting with Rajesh in a Turkish café on Green Lanes. As usual it was jammed with traffic, but back in the day, Rajesh told me, Green Lanes was once the path on which cattle were walked from Hertford to be slaughtered in East London. Often with dogs keeping the animals in line.

Rajesh was born in Dublin and could speak fluent Irish. He had a good ear for languages, but the clarinet, he said, was his first language. He had ordered what was called The Sharing Breakfast. It arrived with three fried eggs for sharing between two, so when I saw her walking down Green Lanes, I took it as a sign that she should join us. I stood up and walked to the window with the idea of offering the third egg to her. Her hair was pulled up in a bun, sealed with a net threaded with tiny red pearls.

Again, her face was obscured by the blue clinical mask stretched across her nose and chin. She was not wearing the trilby because I had her hat. If I was startled to see her, she seemed preoccupied, her attention elsewhere. She was standing near a Turkish bakery called Yasar Halim, staring at the phone in her hand. Perhaps she was lost? There was something defeated in the slope of her shoulders, which upset me because she had been very lively in Athens. It was a cold day and she was wearing a halter-neck top with flared jeans and a jacket draped over her shoulders, a pinstriped jacket with a pink lining that was very like a jacket I myself owned. At one point she took off her mask for three seconds. As if to breathe more easily. In out, in out, in out, and then she put the mask back on.

Rajesh was sitting alone because I was standing by the window. He was tucking into long green peppers, feta pastries, a salad of cucumber, olives, tomatoes, halloumi.

What's going on, Elsa?

I keep seeing that woman, I replied.

Do you know her?

I saw her in Athens.

Why don't you go outside and say hello? He stuck his spoon into a bowl of honey and began to dribble it on to a chunk of bread.

All I knew was that I must not physically go out on to the street and greet her. I knew she was there, but I didn't want to scare her. I felt that with great urgency. She knew I was there too, but she still refused to look in my direction. I wondered if she might be ashamed of me. Something was happening in the sky. Flocks of pigeons had landed on a rooftop above the bakery. And then they rose in a group above the chimney and flew together to another roof. They were not happy there either. No one noticed the distressed birds on the roof because they were looking ahead of them. But she was looking upwards and I was looking at where she was looking.

I've got your hat, I said to her in my head. When you return the horses I will give it back to you.

It's not a matter of returning the horses, she replied. Just because you want them doesn't mean you can have them. Her voice was subdued. Flat. She walked towards a shop that sold gold wedding jewellery and gazed indifferently at the bracelets, rings and necklaces.

So, how's it going? Rajesh asked, even though I had my back to him. Oh fine, could you pass the bread, thanks. I was still standing by the window. He was passing the bread and various jams to someone who wasn't there, to an empty space. The trilby lay on the chair next to him.

Shops had put out their rubbish in black bin liners all along Green Lanes. At night the city foxes, who I knew could make at least twenty-seven different sounds, would come out to search for food to feed their cubs. There were also clinical masks, blue, black, pink, lying discarded by lamp posts and the locked-up bicycles. Everyone had become used to them. The masks were soaked through with spit and snot. Some people referred to masks as muzzles and refused to wear them. Perhaps she wasn't my double after all. She had no energy in her body. When she disappeared in the direction of Turnpike Lane, I decided it was a case of mistaken identity.

Finally, I sat down.

So, you don't want to say hello to her then?

I shook my head.

By the way, Rajesh said, ahem, this is a sharing breakfast. So far, I have been sharing it with myself. What's it like to be back in London?

I told him about why I was sacked from my job in Poros. He laughed for about two minutes and then he laughed again for twelve seconds. Tears ran down his cheeks. He wiped them away with the starched white napkin.

What the hell, Elsa? I mean, Isadora Duncan was ridiculous.

She had to be, I replied, she was making

something new. She was the mother of modern dance.

And then I told him about the ants running around the rim of the bath in my London flat. There was a nest somewhere in the bathroom. Every day these ants ran in purposeful lines around me as I bathed. There was nothing for them to eat except soap, shampoo, toothpaste. Rajesh suggested I buy three ant traps. The ants would run into the poisoned nectar bait inside the trap and proceed to poison the nest. I listened but didn't really feel motivated. Then you have to find out where they are coming from and seal the entry, he said. It was as if the ants had found a portal to my world. The horses were a portal to another world, too.

Maybe they are not.

Maybe they are not what?

A portal. That world is inside you anyway.

I wanted to continue this conversation with her, but we had lost reception on Green Lanes.

*

I told Rajesh that since I had messed up the Rach I found myself leaving the flat and then turning around and walking home to check I had turned off the gas hob. He said he did similar things. At the moment he was worried that his fridge would blow up. Why was that? It was making a wailing sound at night. He was also devastated about his weight gain. During lockdown, he couldn't stop eating. Every day he panged for carbohydrates. Scones, soda bread, crumpets, biscuits of all kinds, particularly the cardamom biscuits sold at the Indian sweet shop near Turnpike Lane. In fact during the first lockdown, in between practising Schubert's Serenade for Clarinet and Piano, he had found a grocery store that supplied his favourite hot cross buns every day of the year.

Don't talk about Schubert, I winced.

It's very soothing to play when people are dying in your street, he replied, but anyway, he resented the endless supply of those Easter buns. Time had become weird enough in the pandemic. His big moments in the major lockdown were cooking the evening meal and eating it in the bath.

Why the bath?

I watched films in the bath as well. Do you think I've got fat?

The buttons of his shirt were straining and his belly flopped over his waistband.

No, I said, not at all.

Anyway, he continued, what I really missed in the lockdowns was buying a coffee. Sipping a flat white. If my identity is so fragile it depends on a flat white to keep it together, I can't see the point of those years I've spent reading difficult theory and philosophy. Capitalism sold a flat white to me as if it were a cup of freedom.

Now that he had no work, he shopped for his elderly neighbours, Alizée and Paul, which was a relief. It gave some structure to his day and made him feel useful, but it upset him too. They had endured a long marriage, sixty years together, their hands always entwined, finishing each other's sentences, predicting each other's needs.

His other neighbours were into astrology and heroin. They told him his lucky colours were purple and gold, his harmony numbers three and nine, his lucky bird was a vulture. But where did that leave him, alone with his clarinet, alone with his wailing fridge and the all-season hot cross buns, no vultures to be found in Salisbury Road.

And he could no longer fit into his trousers.

Who would have sex with a depressed, overweight raisin-bun addict? He didn't even want to have sex with himself. When he sometimes tried to charm his penis into ecstasy, it didn't want to know. Meanwhile, he said, look at the guys in this Turkish restaurant, chopping peppers to grill on skewers later that evening. Someone else was slicing tomatoes, cucumbers and onions for the salads and it was only 9.30 UK time. It was a good feeling, Rajesh said, pointing to the men in their white aprons dissecting half a lamb that had been laid out on a marble slab, to see this preparation for the evening meal, even though he was a vegetarian – all right, he did eat fish, but at least it didn't have hooves.

Some days he thought it was the end of the world, but haven't generations before us always thought that? Also, he was missing his ex-wife.

You mean Bella, I interrupted.

Yes, Bella, he agreed. The way she made him feel loved in the beginning, the way she made him feel unloved towards the end, but he would do up the buttons of her coat any day. He missed her and he would hold an umbrella over her head in the rain. Really, he wished he had handled things better with Bella, but when the ammunition was flying it was hard to be a statesman and make peace, the wounds were too deep and they had met so young, when he was even more stupid than he was now. I did not tell him that Bella was enjoying as much sex and wine as she could bear in Athens.

Rajesh wanted to know who I was teaching next. A sixteen-year-old in Paris. Her name was Aimée. I was to stay in an empty apartment belonging to her grandmother.

It's good you've got some work abroad, he said, but frankly, why don't you set up a summer school in a chateau in Europe and employ us all? I'm broke as hell.

I was about to tell him Bella's message about him paying her back six months of their mortgage, but again decided against it.

We talked about Arthur. Rajesh reminded me of the time he still conducted. How, after he finished a concert, his assistant would pass him a glass of Bénédictine and a cigarette backstage.

He walks every day and he's very fit for a man of eighty, I told Rajesh. Sardinia suits him. He likes the sun. He likes the wine. He has very conservative tastes in food. Apparently, his next-door neighbour, Andrew, is English. He cooks Arthur shepherd's pie and then freezes it so he can heat it up himself at night. Italian cuisine is completely lost on Arthur. This neighbour also sorts out his electricity. It's run from a generator and goes off all the time.

What took him to Sardinia in the first place?

He says love is more possible in the south.

He's preposterous.

For all those reasons I love him, I said.

I showed Rajesh a postcard from Arthur that had just arrived for me in my London flat.

*Send me your sanitized hands so I can hold
them against my old heart.*

Don't read his postcards, Rajesh said. He's
mad. It's well known. Dust yourself off and get
up on stage again. Everyone knows you are a
queen.

Maybe I am.

What shall we do with the eggs?

There it was, our sharing breakfast. Rajesh
had eaten one of them. Two eggs to spare.

Rajesh polished another one off with the rest
of the bread. Have a good time in Paris, he said,
love you.

What's the point in saying *love you* and
leaving out the *I*?

Perhaps that's what had got to Bella.

The waiter arrived with the bill and I put on
the trilby.

I'll look after this, I told Rajesh.

He made some vaguely sorrowful noise
about sharing the bill. If this was how he talked

to his penis, no wonder it was reluctant to be charmed.

Thank you, he said, I'll cook you lunch on Christmas Day.

The last egg lay on the platter, shiny and untouched. Like the Steinway piano in my London ground-floor apartment. The night before, I had placed a sheet over this piano and then I laughed because it reminded me of Vass telling me he had caught a mermaid and tied her in his nets before she could enchant him.

Maybe you should.

Maybe I should what?

Only laugh and smile if you mean it.

The woman who had bought the horses had come through again. Sometimes she wanted to wipe the smile off my face.

By the way, Rajesh tried to sound casually indifferent, did you see Bella in Athens?

Yes, for about five minutes.

He now had a fork in his hand, which reminded me I had brought him a present from Greece.

I've got something for you, I said and, digging into the pocket of my green raincoat, I gave him one of the urchins I had dived for with Vass. It was now just a skeleton, a shell, no needles alive and quivering. Perhaps it resembled the present state of his dead marriage.

I also have a little gift for you to take to Paris. Rajesh lifted something out of his tote bag, which had the name of a vape shop written across its centre. It seemed to be a plug. With a little fan heater attached to it. A travelling heater. He leaned his head against my shoulder and began to explain how it worked.

I love you, Rajesh, I said, and I meant it.

The waiter started to clear our sharing breakfast. We stayed where we were, his head resting against my shoulder while he spoke again of the animals that once walked from Hertfordshire through Green Lanes on their way to slaughter. In those days, he said, we would have heard the sawing and hammering of stonemasons, carpenters and blacksmiths. Also, probably, the rattling of carts and wagons over cobblestones. We looked out of the window at the shoppers on the high street. The worst of the pandemic was over, but everyone looked dazed and battered. A teenage girl waiting at the traffic lights was eating a candy snake. She had its head gripped between her teeth. By the time the lights turned green, its body had more or less disappeared into her mouth. Except for the end of the tail.

I thought again about the man in Athens who had sold the dancing horses to the woman who was very like myself. How he had explained that to start the dance she had to lift up their tails and to stop it she must pull the tails down.

Yet this young woman was eating the tail.

12

I had an hour to wait before boarding the Eurostar to Paris. The raw red bricks and high domed ceiling of London St Pancras International on the Euston Road were graceful and calming. Tracey Emin's installation, *I Want My Time With You*, flowed in pink neon letters across the bricks, and near it, a life-size bronze statue of a man and woman embracing. People had started to travel again. I watched passengers walking around the station's shopping strip, most of them trailing their wheelies. Some carried rucksacks, a few pushed heavy, bulging suitcases. Anyone with a large suitcase looked more forlorn and burdened than those with portable luggage. As far as I could see, we were travellers, customers, tourists. The key to my London flat was safely zipped into the side of my purse. I knew where I kept the butter and light bulbs, the bubble bath and bread knife and the little pebble with a hole in it. Yet, it seemed to me that at any moment, reality could flip. Floods and droughts and wars would see us carrying our mattresses and blankets to the train station, maybe with one small object for luck. If it was the end of the world, would my birth mother want to find me? I gazed at the bronze statue and tried to work out if the embrace was a hello or a goodbye.

After a while, I sat on the stool by one of the pianos that had been donated to the station, a scratched and battered, out-of-tune Yahama. My fingers found the keys and I began to play the piano sections of Rachmaninov's Piano Concerto No. 2. It was not easy to honour Rach's control of tone or crisp playing on the Yamaha, nor his fastidious use of pedals. I could feel the power of his thundering left hand in my left hand. Passengers with time to spare gathered around the piano as I let Rach confide in me again.

Some of them filmed me on their phones. A man wearing a yellow bow tie sat on the floor near the piano and put on the socks he had just purchased.

I played for about sixteen minutes before I slammed down the lid of the battered piano and bowed to the applauding crowd. It was time to go through security.

As I was unzipping my bag to find my passport, a woman of about fifty walked towards the piano and presented me with a bunch of sunflowers. From the wrapping, I saw she had bought them from the expensive florist on the strip. She told me that on Thursdays and Fridays she travelled to London from Margate to work in a supermarket. She was waiting for her train home. The Rachmaninov had moved her beyond, she said. It had even made her forget she was alive.

The piano was situated just opposite Le Pain Quotidian café, which, I suppose, translated as Daily Bread. I thanked her for the flowers, which I knew would have cost her more than she earned in an hour at the supermarket.

When the Departures screen told us the trains to Brussels Midi, Dover Priory, Paris Nord and Margate were on time, she fumbled in her bag for a mask. I gave her two of my own. There was something like the idea of love in the air between us. This dimension of this sort of love, as I understood it, was our understanding, unspoken, of her wish and my wish, and Rachmaninov's wish, to transcend the pain of daily life. Before we parted she told me her name was Ann, without an *e*.

My name is Elsa.

Of course, I know you are Elsa M. Anderson. She started to laugh. I just can't believe I'm talking to you. She scrolled down her phone to show me her photographs of 'the concert' I had just played.

I could not confide in Ann, as I had just let Rachmaninov confide in me. Why would I tell her that I was once Ann without an *e* before Arthur changed my name? I wanted to. I wanted to tell her that Ann had disappeared and returned to earth as Elsa.

Of course I bloody know who you are, Ann said again.

I wiped the dust from the keys of the Yamaha off my fingers. Ann was convinced she knew who I was, but I did not know who I was.

I would have to read the documents. Even then I would not be as sure as she seemed to be. I was flipping all over the place. Ann was waiting for a train at London St Pancras, but five-year-old Ann, who was also myself, was waiting for something too. Waiting for something she wanted very much. Not just wanted but yearned for, would be forever bereft by its absence. What was she waiting for?

A piano, probably.

As if I wouldn't know you, Ann was laughing again, my cousin has all your albums.

What was Ann of Suffolk waiting for?

She was waiting for the tractor at the end of the field to make its way towards her childhood house. A trailer had been attached to the tractor and standing on it was the piano, the small Bösendorfer grand that would replace the piano that had disappeared. It was covered with a cloth but I, she, could clearly see its shape. There was a problem with the tractor's engine. It kept starting and stopping, moving forwards and then stalling. Perhaps it was stranded in the field and the piano would never arrive? I felt her panic enter me once again, under the dome of London St Pancras station.

Goodbye, Elsa. Ann flung her arms around me.

The sunflowers were confiscated at security. The official insisted I could not bring plants to France for planting. But they are not for planting, I explained, they are for putting in a vase. No, there were laws about bringing in pests. I asked her to keep the flowers but they were thrown in a bin. When I eventually boarded the Eurostar and had found my seat, I thought again about Ann. Next to the field that backed on to my childhood house in Suffolk was another field, ablaze with sunflowers.

13

PARIS, NOVEMBER

The Boulevard Saint-Germain apartment looked over the Thursday market on Place Maubert. As I punched in the door code to enter, my phone started to ring. The words *DOOR CALLING* flashed on my screen. It was the new intercom system in my London flat. Someone was trying to get into the building, perhaps it was a delivery. I pressed the hashtag key which opened the door in London. At exactly the same time, I was opening the apartment building door in Paris. I could hear the robot voice in London saying *Please Enter* and the click of the door opening in Paris. It was a strange first doubling.

The small lift to floor five smelled of urine. Maybe there were residents in this smart, bourgeois apartment block who liked to pee in it. It took a while to unlock the front door to my flat with a key that resembled a screwdriver. I had to press it into the lock and then plunge it further in again, not once but twice, and then again, as if it were a door with fathomless depths and the key was having sex with it. At one point it fell to the floor and I had to start all over again.

It was an airy, light apartment. The walls were painted white, wooden floors, a table with six chairs tucked beneath it, a fireplace surrounded by veined grey marble. No piano. These past few months were the first time in my adult life I had lived without a piano, but oddly, the bathroom was wallpapered with sheet music from Beethoven's *Pathétique*. I felt comforted to see it. He had written the *Pathétique* when he was twenty-seven. The age he first realized he was becoming deaf.

The second doubling happened when I took a bath and discovered ants were running across the rim of the bath. They were joyful, fast, they had intention and purpose. There were ants running across the edges of the Parisian bath and the London bath. They had found a portal to all my worlds.

Along with Beethoven's glorious chords and despairing first movement.

My friend Marie walked over to see me an hour later. She was a retired professor of maths and music and had moved to Paris three years ago. We first met at a party after a concert at the Kennedy Center in New York when I was twenty-seven, Beethoven's age when Sonata No. 8 was first published. Marie's hair was now silver and cut short. She was slim, small and clever. When I last saw her in New York she had black curly hair. She told me she had lived through the worst months of the pandemic in Rue Saint-André des Arts. Every day she bought Lebanese bread, made in the restaurant opposite her apartment. On Fridays she cooked fish in red peppercorns. Those were her rituals during The Confinement, as well as the hour she was allowed to leave her apartment for exercise.

We sat on the tiny balcony overlooking the market at Place Maubert and ate the croissants she had bought at her favourite boulangerie, Maison Isabelle.

It's just there, she said, pointing across the square.

So you've gone silver, I said.

She told me that silver represents the person she became internally before she cut her hair.

This is my truth, she continued. Do we become someone and then set about visually making that person? I have accepted the evolution of my life on earth. I am seventy years old.

Right, I replied.

Marie told me what she thought about my blue hair.

You had to create yourself, she said.

We all have to do that, I replied to Marie.

My words were smaller than my feelings at that moment. I had spent my life finding diplomatic words. Am I a diplomat then? Isn't it hard enough to play Beethoven?

As it happens, Marie continued, you look thin and pale.

I told her about the audience demanding a refund for the concert I had messed up in Vienna.

Really, you have been Arthur's hostage, she said.

Like everyone else she wanted to know why I was not at least teaching at the conservatoire where the students were serious musicians.

Elsa, every conservatoire in the world would be pleased to have you. You would be paid properly. No one can understand it. You are a personage, a celebrity.

Maybe I am.

The Thursday market was closing down. A team of men in orange jackets were cleaning the square with a powerful hosepipe. The man who sat begging outside the boulangerie was busy moving to the other side of the road with his bags and blankets. When I watched him gather his belongings, I did not feel disconnected to him, more the other way around. Sometimes I wondered if those men living rough were related to me. I didn't want him to be connected to me, but it was a possibility. I could not bring myself to not see him, which is how most people I knew coped with rough sleepers.

Marie told me about a swimming pool that was nearer my apartment than the Joséphine Baker.

Piscine Pontoise.

I made a note of the address while she started to talk about all the famous women who had committed suicide by drowning. There are vertical swimmers and horizontal swimmers, she said. I myself have sometimes thought I will become a vertical swimmer. No one says I have to do the third act of my life. It is always nasty. If I become ill in old age, I have not ruled it out.

Really?

Of course. No one rules it out. Ask anyone on this boulevard and they will tell you they have considered it. Pills. Rope. Gun. Weed-killer. Water. Jumping off high buildings.

The conversation had taken a strange turn. I wondered if Marie had spent too much time alone in the pandemic.

Look, she said, it's a taboo subject because it's true. We all think about ways of ending life. It's a thought experiment and what's wrong with that?

With what?

A thought experiment. That's what thoughts do. They don't write manifestos for you to agree with or stroke puppies while munching a bag of M&M's with a friend who loves you unconditionally. Unless the thinker is so fragile she wants to lock them up in the stable and nail a picture of a birthday cake to the door.

While Marie was speaking I played Beethoven's *Pathétique*, Sonata No. 8, in my head.

She was now making weird slicing-her-throat gestures with her hand.

You will agree, Elsa, that most of us don't go through with it, but we have at least walked our minds on this forbidden pasture and let them graze there?

*

Maybe I am.

Maybe you are what?

Standing on the forbidden pasture.

By the way, Marie said, because you wear that hat all the time, your hair is matted and flat. You need to brush it. She had a spare comb in her bag. There were threads of silver hair in the comb. I did not have silver hair internally yet.

A fleet of seven ambulances with sirens blaring raced by on Boulevard Saint-Germain. From my balcony we watched people queuing for cakes at Maison Isabelle. When Marie left, she wished me luck with all that lay ahead.

I had no idea what lay ahead. All I knew was that I would see the woman who had bought the horses again, here in Paris. That night I walked alone on the banks of the Seine. The moon and stars were bright. I let the stars enter my body and realized I had become porous. Everything that I was had started to unravel. I was living precariously in my own body; that is to say, I had not fallen into who I was, or who I was becoming. What I wanted for myself was a new composition. I had let the woman who bought the horses enter me, too.

On the way home I stopped at a hole in the wall, a bar called Onze. It was one small, dark room and I was the only person there. I sat on the stool by the counter while the kind gentleman behind the bar – he said he was originally from Algeria – poured me a glass of eau de vie. Made from pears. It is usually sipped after a meal, he told me.

I'd eaten nothing all day except the croissants Marie had brought to my apartment. But that wasn't strictly true. The stars and the Seine were inside me. I was living in a very strange way, but I knew there were people in the world who were also living like this. Someone in Tokyo or Eritrea or New York or Denmark at this very moment was living life precariously, too. This mood, with its ambience of low-level panic and hyper-alert connections to everything, would have its double or echo. I heard its music in my head under my hat. Her hat. It was hard to listen to it, but it was there, like a future that was obscure, a future infected by the governance of the world, the old and new tyrants and their consorts and enablers. I no longer wanted to think about them because they had too much attention anyway. Yet, I thought about them all the time.

And what about my double, who perhaps was not physically identical? To think about her was to speak to someone known, inside myself, someone who was slightly mysterious to me, someone who was listening very attentively.

The barman filled up my glass.

There was still no one in the bar except the man.

And her.

It was cold that evening. Winter was coming in. I had to search for some extra blankets, which I found folded in a cupboard. They smelled of mothballs and dead lavender. I plugged in the tiny fan heater that Rajesh had given me in Green Lanes. This little device, Rajesh had insisted, was the future. It could heat up a whole room at a very low cost. He had bought seven of them at a bargain price. It was switched on but nothing was happening. Eventually, I felt a little heat on my left foot. Perhaps not even the whole foot, just my toes. Birdsong filled the room. I reached for my phone. It was Tomas calling to say we should meet up while we were both in Paris.

14

My student lived in Rue des Écoles in the 5th. Her name was Aimée and she was sixteen. I took the lift to the third floor and heard her playing before I saw her. She was struggling with the first movement of the *Pathétique*. Perhaps her family were obsessed with it? I listened outside the front door while I looked for my mask. She was closed in, tight, playing too fast.

Her mother opened the door.

My daughter is waiting, is all she said.

Aimée's black hair was short and sleek. She wore tight jeans, a white T-shirt, unlaced plimsolls and a surgical mask like my own. She told me she wanted to use her time with me to practise *Trois Gymnopédies*, three pieces for solo piano by French composer Erik Satie. It was for a concert at school. She was just playing the *Pathétique* to get her mother off her back. Sorry, she said, her head was dead today. She had smoked weed with her friend the night before and then they ate sushi. It was probably off and now it was like she had a washing machine in her stomach. To be honest, she said, her mood today was like waiting for a bus on a Sunday night in a deserted street.

Fine, I said, I have only offered two lessons, so let's begin.

Aimée wanted to show off everything she could play. She had a sharp musical mind. Perhaps she became tired too easily.

We will start, I said, not with Satie but with Chopin.

We were going to proceed slowly. I believed in slow practice because it allowed time for thinking. We would practise Chopin's Étude in G-sharp minor, Op. 25, No. 6, at a snail's pace. It usually takes about two minutes to play, but we would work so slowly it would almost become unrecognizable.

It always gives me cramp in the left hand, she complained.

Yes, I replied, Chopin gave the most interesting notes to the left hand.

We would penetrate its composition and pay attention to Chopin's daring fingers.

I was wearing black trousers and a white polo neck. Sometimes I sounded like Arthur. Was Aimée mournful and poised? No, that would be Marcus. Aimée was on edge and furious.

An hour into the lesson her mother sent a tray of cream puff pastries and two Nespressos into the music room. In my telephone conversations with her, she had insinuated that her daughter was mentally fragile, something of a fantasist. She asked me to be discreet in this matter.

Aimée pointed to the plate. These pastries are called millefeuille, she said. It means, in English, the baker had sex on a thousand leaves in the dark forest of Fontainebleau.

I bit into the pastry and ate it with relish. A new greed for all the pastries in France. She lifted her millefeuille off the plate and weighed it in her palm. Ah, she said, so light, so crazy, it's nearly not there. She put it down again on the plate. I often go walking in this forest. If you want to get out of Paris, Fontainebleau is not such a long drive.

She showed me the tattoo on her arm. A heart with an eye in it and there were flames through the heart.

At one point my swimming costume fell out of my bag and she told me about learning to swim in a river in the countryside when she was four. There were fish and weeds. She was nervous because she could not see the bottom of the water and there were currents. She climbed down the ladder and yes, yes, yes, she was in the water and the river was wild and cold. It was, she said, a moment. That was Aimée, wild and cold. It was strange to teach a student who was attracted to the melancholy of Satie, a melancholy so deceptively light it was nearly suicidal, yet had no internal conversation with the composer she loved. I admired her because she did not consider the printed note sacred. She knocked back her coffee and threw her cup on the floor. She was all swagger, but she was not that interested in music. When I was her age I had no life outside of my instrument; nothing interested me more. Every day I accomplished something on the piano that was nearly impossible. I had to accept there were different reasons for learning to play an instrument. I listened to Aimée and thought that like Marcus, she was playing to get away from her parents. Perhaps at her age I was playing to get closer to the parent I never knew.

We continued with the Chopin étude. Twelve minutes in, she ripped off her mask.

I hate this fucking thing, she said. It's ruining my life. Satie would never write an étude or a sonata, he invented a new genre. I'm not doing this shit.

Her voice was hard but her lips were soft. She kept a little flask of water by the piano and a bottle of perfume that smelled of figs.

One thing is for sure, she said in French, I will never write a symphony to thank my family for all the happiness they have given me.

It didn't surprise me that she had chosen

Satie's *Gymnopédies* for her school concert. Satie worked against classical harmonies and structures, and Aimée was against everything too. She told me she would wear a velvet trouser suit on the day of the concert. Satie owned seven velvet suits and wore them in rotation every day of his life. In her view the dresses I wore for my concerts – she had scrutinized them on YouTube – were so old school, she wondered who I was trying to please. In fact, she said, the only thing that would make them less pathetic was to insert a small hammer into the lining of the most dismal of the dresses. After all, Satie carried a hammer around with him at all times for protection.

Right, I said, when you practise a *Gymnopédie*, break it down into sections like we did with the Chopin and add your own phrasing. They're easy to play, so why do you need me?

You are my hammer, she said.

Who do you need protecting from?

Everyone.

She slammed the lid of the piano and told me I was dismissed.

What are you going to do when I leave?

I will make love with George Sand to get closer to Chopin, she said, sinking her teeth into the millefeuille.

On the way out, her mother asked me if I was happy with her daughter's progress.

Yes, I replied, she is very sensible and hard-working.

15

I next saw the woman who had bought the horses at Café de Flore. This time it was definitely her. It was Arthur who insisted I go to the Flore before I went to the pharmacy for my vaccination. It will be warmer than your bedroom, he said. It has a powerful coal stove and you can make your coffee last all day. His voice had become weak and shaky. You should know, he whispered, that the philosopher will be working there. He has made the first floor of this café his office. I hear the management have given him his own telephone line so he can take calls.

After a while I realized he was serious. It was the first time I thought Arthur might have dementia. The philosopher he was referring to was

Jean-Paul Sartre, whose grave I had recently visited in Montparnasse. His mind was wandering all over the place in this call. At one point he called me Ann rather than Elsa. He had never made that slip before. In fact his neighbour, Andrew, who seemed to be with him every day, had taken the phone from him. Andrew spoke English with a northern accent. He told me Arthur was tired and needed to rest. His voice was tense, maybe even hostile. I could hear Arthur demanding his phone be returned to him. At one point he shouted, Who are you? I wasn't sure if he was referring to me or his neighbour.

I managed to get a table on the pavement of Café de Flore opposite Brasserie Lipp and ordered a Perrier mixed with mint syrup. I had first seen this fairy-green drink in the South of France and had always wanted to taste it. An elderly gentleman at the table next to me pierced his potato with a knife and lifted it to his eyes. His false lower teeth jutted out of his mouth. He was a little breathless.

I suppose I was thinking about Arthur. I was confused about my responsibility for his well-being. He had adopted me in order to teach me. We had an entirely professional relationship. But I had been six years old. He had employed various au pairs over the years and a cook, so it was never all that clear if he was my father or my teacher or both. I had never shared my secret thoughts or anxieties with Arthur.

Two men sitting at the table behind me asked if I'd take their photo. They were in their twenties and tucking into plates of croque-monsieur. Both wore T-shirts and identical black leather jackets. The man on the right, who had chiselled cheekbones, handed me his phone. I asked where he was from.

Dresden, he said.

Rachmaninov composed his Piano Concerto No. 2 in Dresden. It was where he and his family lived for four years from 1906. He was depressed, devastated, at first unable to write anything at all. When he finally finished it, his sadness lifted. He dedicated this mighty work to his doctor.

Do you know Dresden? he said.

Maybe I do.

I asked them to move in closer together for the photo. This seemed impossible for the man who had given me his phone, but his friend on the left moved in, draping his arm around the shoulder of the man from Dresden.

I took three photos and returned the phone. The Perrier-menthe arrived. It was a strange taste. Maybe like liquid toothpaste. While I was checking my emails on my phone, the man from Dresden tapped me on the shoulder. I turned around. He bent his face towards me and whispered in English, I want to lick you.

It was at that moment I saw her walking down Boulevard Saint-Germain towards Café de Flore.

She was wearing the same brown shoes with the curved snakeskin heels she had worn in Athens. My first thought was that I was wearing her trilby hat. This time she was not wearing a mask. Yet it was not her face I was focusing on, it was her mouth. Perched between her lips was a fat cigar. Glowing at the end. It was a poke at life. A provocation. It was if she was wreathed in a transparent cloud. She had attitude and confidence. Her hair was dark brown, piled in a loose bun on top of her head.

Voluptuous.

Curves.

Hips. Belly.

A white silk pleated dress. A thick gold belt.

Her hands were entirely free, no bags, she carried nothing but herself down Boulevard Saint-Germain. Like the ants in Paris and London she was walking fast and with purpose. Perhaps she was perfectly composed. Self-composed. She saw me. Our eyes locked. I realized I was terrified. For a moment she looked truly shocked, too. Our mutual fear was identical. She and I had the same expression in our eyes. And then she slowed down right by my table. Mingling with the smell of the cigar was the fragrance of geraniums. With her brown eyes still locked on my green eyes, she whipped the cigar out of her mouth and threw it into my glass of Perrier-menthe. It was a message. There you are, wearing my hat. And then she started to run. Fast. In her snakeskin heels, scattering the pigeons on the pavement. There was a wind up that day and the pleats of her white silk dress fanned out so that I thought she might take off into the sky, like a hot-air balloon. Yet she was no angel or ghost, she was totally alive and vital. I stood up and ran after her, just as she turned left into Rue Saint-Benoît. She had taken my horses after all. But she was too fast for me, even in her snakeskin heels. I couldn't see her anywhere. I stopped to get my breath back outside a jazz club in the same road. For a moment, I thought I glimpsed her leaning against a car, reading a book. It was not her. I was now out of breath, gasping, my hands holding on tight to her hat on my head.

When I returned to my table at Flore, I felt weirdly elated. Her cigar was still smouldering in my glass of Perrier-menthe. As if to prove she was not an apparition, that she lived in this city and now she knew I did too. The two men in identical leather jackets were drinking large glasses of beer. It was strange because they made no eye contact with me, but the one from

Dresden who had said *I want to lick you* looked sly and sheepish. It was as if he wanted to scare me, or to excite me, or to show me he was more interested in women than men after his friend put his arm around his shoulder. I think he was expecting me to respond, to reply in some way, but I didn't care about him or his problems. She had my attention. He was not the centre of my world. That was the old composition and I had walked out of that world.

I had literally walked off the stage.

16

On my way to the pharmacy in Boulevard Saint-Michel I noticed I was walking as she had walked. With purpose and composure. Maybe even self-composure, but I wouldn't go that far. No. An impersonation of self-composure. The pharmacist was waiting for me, a young woman called Alice. She wore a white medical coat. After we had gone through all the administration, she stood up and walked to a small fridge where the vaccine was stored.

We will make a little piece of history, she said. Un petit morceau d'histoire.

She wanted to know, given I was a pianist, which arm would be best for the needle, left or right? I chose the left arm. After all, it was with the right arm that I lifted my glass of eau de vie at Onze.

I rolled up my sleeve and she dabbed at my left arm with cotton wool.

One, two, three, here we go, she said.

The needle was in my arm. The vaccine was inside my body, like my passport number was inside her computer. Alice stuck a small round plaster over the pinprick of blood. Thank you, Alice, I said, you have made a piece of history. I kept the receipt, the batch number and the name of the vaccine. I also bought a tube of orange-flower hand cream.

When I arrived at my apartment block on Boulevard Saint-Germain, there was a note stuck on the front door of the building. It was not addressed to me, but it was for me. Apparently, I had left my phone at Flore. In sloping writing, the person who had found it had written an address in Boulevard Saint-Michel, which was where I had just been. Not the pharmacy end, but closer to the Luxembourg Gardens. I searched my bag. It was true, my phone was not inside it.

Was the note from the horse woman or the man who wanted to lick me?

I asked the concierge if I could use her phone and called Marie. She walked over and we agreed we would walk together to the address on the note.

Do you think it's true that you left your phone on the table in Flore? She was wearing heavy black boots because she'd been sweeping broken glass from the doorway of her apartment.

I thought it was possible.

So how does this person know where you live?

I had taped my address on the back of my phone on the Eurostar.

You must be careful, Elsa. You are famous. Everyone wants a piece of you.

I had not told her about the woman who had bought the horses. Perhaps she would open the door and then what would happen? What if she bartered? I will give you your phone if you give me my hat. And then she would keep the horses.

The building was an old bourgeois apartment block opposite a big bookshop. I pressed the numbers written on the note and we waited. Eventually the door clicked open.

No, Marie said, whoever has your phone must come down.

I pressed the code again. The door clicked.

Is there anything on your phone you can't live without?

My banking apps, I said. I wanted to say, *Arthur, I can't live without Arthur*, but decided not to in case Marie started to rant.

We could hear someone walking down the stairs. Softly. Slowly. Softly. Faster.

And then a thud. As if she had jumped over the last four stairs.

It was obviously her.

My left arm was hurting from the jab. It felt heavy and it ached.

Would I give her the hat and take my phone? No. I wanted the horses more than I wanted the phone. The tail was up. The dance had begun.

It's getting cold, Marie said. November in Paris can be brutal.

We heard a click and the heavy door opened.

It was the man who wanted to lick me.

At first he didn't notice Marie, small, silver and seventy. He held my phone in his hand. I thanked him and he started to wave it around as if he were conducting an imaginary orchestra. He was barefoot and he seemed sleepy and he was smirking. Every time I stretched out my hand he would make to give it to me, almost touching the palm of my hand, and then he whipped it away. Eventually he held it above his head and asked for two hundred euro. Marie stepped forwards and his eyes flicked towards her for the first time. Too late. She slammed her heavy boot on to his bare foot with such force that he jumped and yelled with pain. The phone fell from his hand and I grabbed it.

Fuck you, whores, he shouted, and then all the usual. We were queers, we were freaks, we were Jews, we were hags, we were ugly, we were mad. The same old composition. Eventually, red in the face, he slammed the door.

He's from Dresden, I told Marie, which is

where Rachmaninov wrote some of Piano Concerto No. 2.

Maybe he *is* Rachmaninov, Marie said.

We went off to celebrate at the Vietnamese near Place Maubert, and sat at a table on the sunken pavement. Marie showed me the heavy silver rings she had bought in Morocco. They had markings, words on the sides, but she didn't know what they meant. She said she would have to return home straight after dinner because her lover was arriving from Nice that evening. We ate tofu and sticky rice, prawn-dumpling soup and drank tap water. And then I saw her shadow on the sunken pavement and I could smell cigar smoke. Without turning around, I knew it was her. She was with her elderly male companion, the man who had been with her in Athens. Stooped, silent, brooding.

I could see his shadow too. This time I did not run after her, because I knew her male companion was too old to run.

It was as if he were her shield.

I let her be there and she let me be there. We

had made some sort of peace with each other. There was something like the idea of an understanding in the air, but I did not know what we had agreed to understand.

After a while I decided to tell Marie that I had a double following me around the world.

I possibly saw her in London, definitely in Athens and now in Paris.

Where is she now?

I never know where she is.

So she has disappeared?

No, she comes back. I saw her shadow when we were eating tonight.

But you want to see her?

I stole her hat and she knows it.

Marie wanted to know how I was feeling after the jab.

My arm was sore but I felt fine. She didn't believe me and insisted on walking me home. I punched in the door code and it didn't work, so I tried replacing the six with an eight.

Run the code past me, Marie said, I am a professor of maths. I shook my head and tried again. A sudden loud blast of cheering came from the café opposite the apartment. A big crowd had gathered around a screen to watch a football match. When I told Marie she should go and leave me to sort it out, she said she was not going anywhere until I was safely inside my flat.

How little we know of the body, Marie intoned. How little we know about science or how the economy works or why Elsa M. Anderson has stopped performing.

She stepped away from the door to give me some space to remember the code. A woman was riding her electric scooter at high speed on the pavement. She had AirPods in her ears and nearly ran Marie over. Holy smoke!

Marie looked infuriated. She took off one of the heavy rings she had bought in Morocco and threw it at the scooter woman's head. It was a good shot because the heavy metal bounced against the back of her skull and fell into the gutter.

It's okay for you, Elsa, Marie said. You're nearly six foot in flat shoes, no one would dare run you over.

I ran towards the gutter and bent down to look for her ring.

My God, Marie, you must have cut her head.

A thread of red blood gleamed on the metal. I wrapped my cardigan over my fingers, picked it up and brought it to her. The ring looked like an extracted tooth, bleeding and raw.

Marie wiped the ring with her handkerchief. Shame I didn't knock her head off.

She was not in the mood to be literally run over, she said, her lover was emotionally running her over every day. She told me that what had been transmitted to her by Julia, who was returning from Nice to see her this evening, was that Julia was in love with everyone and everyone was in love with Julia. Marie required her lover to be more particular in her affections.

I was now frantically trying out new number combinations, none of which was correct. The door remained firmly closed.

Go and meet Julia, it will come back to me.

I think there's a four and a six in your code, she said, try that.

She started to make small talk while I tried another combination.

It's a fact, Marie said, that during the various

lockdowns the whole world was busy rewilding itself. Wasn't there a herd of giraffes rampaging through Kilburn, North-west London? And what about the ostriches on Peckham Common?

I wanted her to go away so I could rewild my memory. Ever since I had confessed to her the various sightings of my double, she seemed to have become protective and sly.

Try two-four-eight-six.

I did as she suggested and the door clicked open.

How did you know that?

The numbers that are shiny are the number that are touched the most often. So obviously those numbers are part of the code.

She hugged me and finally walked off with the bloody ring in her pocket.

Later that evening, while I was making a pot of ginger tea, it seemed to me there was too much heat coming from the tiny ring of gas on the hob. It felt as if my face was bent over a roaring log fire.

I couldn't work it out. I lowered the blue

flame under the pot of ginger and then I realized the heat was coming from myself. My face was burning up. When I looked in the mirror my cheeks were red and so was my chest. I had a headache. My heart was racing. I took two paracetamol and carried the tea to bed. After a while I opened the doors to the little wrought-iron balcony. It was midnight. I placed my laptop on the circular table and sat down on the chair.

The moon was bright. The air was cool. I was hot. My laptop was making a sound. It was a Skype call from Marie. Why was she calling me at midnight on Skype? I took the call. She was wearing a sleeveless black dress, and when she turned to pick something up from the floor, I saw it was unzipped at the back.

How are you, Elsa?

I told her I thought I had *it*.

She asked me about my symptoms. I explained how I had a fever and headache. No, she said, it's just the side effects from the vaccine.

It was odd that she was calling me at this time. It was even odder that she had started to pour oil into the icon lamp on her wall.

Are you religious, Marie?

Not at all.

I had recently watched Carl Theodor Dreyer's *The Passion of Joan of Arc*, in which Joan is asked by the judge if God has made her promises. That's what I asked Marie.

Has God made you promises?

She thought about this on my screen as the moon moved behind a cloud.

Yes, God has made me promises.

Do you talk to God?

Her cheeks were flushed and I knew she'd just had sex.

I definitely have a conversation going with God. It's like a ventriloquist, my voice split into two voices. I think the main promise God has made is Death will not come for me.

This was confusing because earlier she had spoken about ending her life before she was too old to make her own decisions.

Yes, well, it's two contradictory thoughts, she said, the possibility of ending my life and wanting more life. So what? And here are two more contradictions: I don't believe in God, but

I talk to something like God. I ask this presence to feel for me when I have cut down my own feelings.

I told her that Arthur, who was a committed atheist, had often quoted a letter from William Blake. I think he said it was from the diaries, he didn't know.

Dear Father, dear Mother, the church is cold,
But the Ale-house is healthy & pleasant &
warm.

Arthur is a dick, she replied.

There was someone in the apartment with her. I could hear the sound of a radio in the room, a commentary about a horse race.

Yeah, Marie said, there's a rumour that a mysterious woman is lying in my bed and she's listening to the races.

What, even at midnight?

Especially at midnight. How are you feeling now?

Not well.

My hand hovered above the leave button.

Don't go. Julia wants to talk to you. Stay there, Elsa. Stay there.

I understood that she had just been filling in time while Julia listened to the result of the races.

A woman walked on to the screen with a bottle of wine in her hand. Her silver hair was swept back into a bubble ponytail. It looked like a string of baubles, sleek and shiny, hanging down her left shoulder.

Hallo, she said. Marie tells me you now teach piano to children?

It was obvious they had just made love and had dressed especially for this call. Julia was wearing low-slung jeans and a Chanel belt. Her mask, a black N95, hung from her wrist. Maybe she had worn it in bed. Marie disappeared from the screen.

Julia told me she had just returned from Nice. She had lots to say about the glittering light on the sea, the statue of Garibaldi in the square by Café de Turin, the salt cod, the bling of the Côte d'Azur. A small black mole floated above her lip.

But Elsa, she said, I have something else to tell you. I was at that concert.

Which concert?

I was there in Vienna. I was there to hear you play Rachmaninov's Piano Concerto Two in the Golden Hall. In fact it was sold out and I was amongst the two hundred people standing.

Julia's voice was soft and low. Her face filled the screen.

It is true that we lost Rachmaninov's second concerto for piano, she said, but for two minutes and twelve seconds we listened to Elsa M. Anderson play something that made us stop breathing.

While she spoke, I looked out at the trees standing above the stone fountain opposite my apartment. Their roots flowing onwards and outwards, spreading under the tarmac of Boulevard Saint-Germain.

There was clearly something happening to our virtuoso, Julia said, frowning now. The man with the baton heard your detour, he could have calmed the orchestra, he could have created silence. You are not a beginner, after all. We could have heard Elsa M. Anderson's first concerto and not Rach's second.

The rough sleepers had made their beds near the stone fountain. It was always my fear that one day I would join them.

We were with you, she continued, but the guy with the baton was in the way, his ego, his big gestures, conducting with his head, playing to the crowd. And when your piano parted from the orchestra, the way he turned around and poked the baton in your direction – it was terrible. Terrible. But we were there for you, not him. We would listen to anything you play.

I watched the traffic flowing over the tarmac of Boulevard Saint-Germain. Underneath it, the roots of trees reaching outwards. A whole world breathing underneath the taxis and night buses. It was true that the conductor had his back to me. He was working for the orchestra in front of him, after all. He had turned around to see what was happening to his pianist. It was true that he began to communicate his dismay to the audience. Not with words, but with gestures. Whirling his baton in a circle near his ears, tapping his own head with the baton, shrugging his shoulders in despair, making the audience laugh. Despite his taunting, my hands refused to play for him.

I took a sip of the ginger tea.

You can't silence a whole orchestra, I said. They have a job to do. They had been rehearsing for months.

Yes, you can, Julia said. He was the man with the baton. It's his job to lead the orchestra. He could have made history. He could have made a space for us to hear you.

After I pressed the leave button in the cold night under the moon of Maubert, I lay in bed and a great fit of sobbing entered my body.

17

Do we have to defend ourselves against love?
Arthur had sent me a message:

*Every day I do not hear you play moves
me closer to deaf.*

I couldn't stop thinking about the deaf
while I carried the rubbish to the bin room, still
weak and shaky after the weeping hours. The
concierge was Portuguese. She lived with her
family in the apartment to the right of the lift.
She wanted to know if I had found my phone.
Yes, a man from Dresden returned it to me, I
said. She looked at the bin liner in my hand. It
was her husband, she told me, who looked after
the bins, but it was important to tie the plastic

in a tight knot because there were mice in the building.

But the mice have teeth, I said. They can get in, even with a tighter knot.

She smiled and shook her head. Yes, but we have to make life more difficult for them. They had become so confident, they were peeing in the lift. She told me she did extra cleaning for some of the flats. There were wealthy people telling her how the pandemic had made everyone aware how people like her were truly valuable.

It had never occurred to her, she said, that she wasn't valuable.

I walked to Odéon to have an antigen test at a pop-up testing tent by the Métro. Rajesh now had the virus. It was a shock, he moaned, to suddenly see two red lines and not one appear on the white rectangle made in China. Best for me to stock up on food. His neighbour, Alizée, had just brought him a pile of calves' liver. Not only was he vegetarian, not only was the cow sacred and so were her children, it was Alizée who had given him Covid in the first place. I was only half listening because I had a headache and couldn't stop sneezing. I would cancel my lesson with Aimée, go to bed, prepare to become breathless, and die.

The test was negative.

On my way to my second and last lesson with Aimée, I passed a statue of Montaigne, the philosopher. Something made me reach out and touch his bronze shoe. It was shiny, so I reckoned other passers-by had done the same thing. Why did we all want to touch his shoe?

It had a strap across the ankle. And a buckle.

Aimée seemed preoccupied and on edge. I asked her what was on her mind. At first, she ignored me and just hammered the piano. I noticed that she had very sharp fingernails. Painted pink. After a while I told her to take a break and I would play the Satie for her, from beginning to end. She seemed excited at this suggestion. I suddenly realized that she admired me.

After the weeping hours the night before, I was touched, moved, by her respect. She even wiped the piano stool down with her cardigan and asked me where I would like her to sit. I told her to pull up a chair and sit with me at the piano. Did she agree that I should play slowly and sorrowfully? Depends, she said, it's more like a question he is asking and doesn't want to know the answer.

While I played *Gymnopédie No. 1* she began to speak. What was on her mind was something to do with her childhood cat. A Siamese. It liked to eat flowers, but most of all it loved mimosa. So she picked her a bunch now and again and the cat would devour the yellow flowers. I think it was like a drug, Aimée said, like a psychedelic. This same cat always slept on Aimée's stomach under the blankets when she was thirteen. In February, when the mimosa was out, she had bronchitis, so the family doctor was called to the apartment. He lifted the blanket to listen to her heart with his cold stethoscope. There was a moment when the stethoscope pressed against her breast. Her nipple, in fact, which was nothing to do with her breathing problem. And then her other breast. Same thing. His stethoscope pressed down. Precisely like before. She could see his excitement. The cat, who had been sleeping on her stomach, leaped up and scratched his face. Three deep welts. He was bleeding from his forehead to his chin. He asked for the cat to be killed.

Someone was knocking on the door. Two knocks. Aimée's mother arrived to tell us the lesson was over and her daughter now had to concentrate on her history homework. We agreed on an extra thirty minutes. During this exchange, this barter for more time, her mother looked at me beseechingly, insinuating with her eyes that her daughter was unhinged. I shut the door and continued to play Satie's most popular composition. Ambient. Ahead of its time. Only loved twenty years after it was written. I took Aimée's interpretation, and while we spoke I played it like a painful question floating through time.

And what if it had been you, I said, who lifted her arms and scratched the doctor's face?

I didn't have to. The cat was my protector.

You mean your cat did what you wanted to do?

Yes.

Where were your parents?

Ah, she laughed, but she didn't mean it. They respect authority, so when a doctor tells them to leave the room, they obey him. Her humour was droll. The doctor told her father he saw the cat in a field when he was driving on the motorway to Normandy. It was stalking sheep, waiting to pounce, a real killer.

What happened to the doctor?

My Siamese scared him away, she said. He did not come again. I heard he died of a heart attack in Le Havre. Her fingers found the keys and she took over from me. I would like a life like yours, she whispered, a life travelling the world to play concerts.

Where was her cat now?

Living with her grandmother in the countryside.

She wanted me to know she had a boyfriend. They went camping last weekend and they smoked weed in the tent and played poker. She was okay, she said, she was on fire because no one believed her. She had been on fire for three years.

And anyway, why do you always wear that hat?

We need to be in D-sharp.

Sorry. She corrected her mistake.

I told her about the dancing horses in Athens and the woman who had bought them. How I was convinced she was a sort of psychic double. Sometimes, I said, she and I are in conversation with each other.

I appreciated the long, cool look Aimée gave me at that moment. Her clear brown eyes making an assessment. How sane or insane was her teacher, who had clearly been weeping all night? Did it matter? She had another question about the woman who had bought the horses:

But why does she speak your thoughts for you?

Well, I said, you will have to ask that question to your cat.

I liked watching Aimée's pretty pink claws on the piano keys.

For the record of history, I turned towards Aimée, I believe you. And I'm pleased the cat was on your side and saw off your predator.

She looked confounded but interested.

You have poured some water on my fire, she said.

I stood up and left her bent over the piano, an Érard, made from polished rosewood.

Did the doctor really ask for the cat to be killed?

No. She looked up at me. That is the only detail I made up.

We laughed for a while. A strange laugh. The release of deep rage.

Suddenly she had a little more kindness in D-sharp.

It's our last lesson and I'm sad, she said. Obviously, I can play the Satie, I just wanted to meet you. What are you going to do tomorrow?

I told her I had a date with a film-maker I met on a boat in Greece.

Whatever you do, Elsa, don't smoke a cigar on this date.

I don't smoke cigars.

You do. I can smell it on your clothes.

Aimée took out her bottle of perfume that smelled of figs and theatrically spritzed it over my wrists.

As I made my way through the hallway, her mother asked me directly about her daughter's state of mind.

Is it true your family doctor died? I asked her back, directly.

Yes, truly, she replied.

You should listen to your daughter.

She told me that she had been listening to her daughter play piano for ever.

No, you need to listen to her words.

I don't like words, she snapped back, that's why I papered the bathroom of my mother's apartment with the *Pathétique*.

18

The last time I saw Tomas we had pulled the tail up to kiss under the stars of Poros. Did I regret pulling it down again? To avoid speaking about awkward things we had slipped our heads under the sea. When we surfaced, we still did not exchange words. We were naked and drunk and confused. While we looked for our clothes on the deserted beach, I found a gold cigarette lighter buried in the sand. It was designed to look like a faux bar of real gold, the word *Champ* carved into its base instead of a hallmark. I kept the lighter as a souvenir. It had a high flame like that evening on Love Bay. And it was gold like treasure found in a shipwreck.

He had booked us a table for lunch at a brasserie in Bastille. I arrived five minutes early.

The pavement directly outside the brasserie was being dug up by men with pneumatic drills, headphones clamped to their ears. It was a battle to get inside the door. I took off my black felt trilby and handed it to the waiter. He hung it on a wooden stand that was vibrating from the impact of the drilling outside. It seemed to be alive with nervous energy in that corner of the brasserie. He apologized for the noise and pointed to our reserved table. A glass of champagne on the house, he said, would be with me soon.

When Tomas walked in, he slapped his hands over his ears and suggested we eat somewhere else. We discussed it like an old married couple, but when the waiter arrived with two glasses of free champagne, we became strangers again and decided to stay.

Tomas ordered twelve oysters and two urchins, which he said would remind us of our boat trip in Poros.

He was more at ease in his adopted city. An orchid poked out of his jacket buttonhole. He told me that he had taken on a small extra job.

It was good to have a break from the documentary on Agnès Varda. He had agreed to direct a twelve-minute film about Marcel Proust's bedroom. To get into the spirit of Proust, who wore a fresh orchid in his buttonhole every day, he sometimes bought a fresh orchid too, but only when he had a rendezvous with someone for whom he had affection and warm feelings.

We clinked glasses.

I asked Tomas what was special about Proust's bedroom.

It was lined with cork tiles because of his asthma and allergies. The cork helped to prevent pollen and dust. And of course, Tomas grimaced, it soundproofed the room. Perhaps this brasserie should tile the walls with cork, too?

The drilling had stopped for a while.

I ordered us a bottle of wine, a Muscadet, which the waiter explained was from where the Loire Valley meets the Atlantic. When I was last in a pub in London, the waiter had described the wine I'd chosen as farm-y. Did he mean it tasted like mud? It's a natural wine, he had said vaguely.

The drilling had started again and no one could hear anybody else.

Tomas continued the conversation, raising his voice, but I just heard the word *technology*.

What did you say about technology?

There's a program, he said, where you can sample a voice recording of a famous person and then write a script and the whole script can be narrated in the real voice of that person.

He was trying to find, without success, a voice recording of Proust.

I told him it was wrong to use Proust's own voice. He wanted to know why.

You've stolen his actual voice. It's one thing to put your thoughts into his mouth, but not in his own voice.

Well, you and I don't agree on this subject, Tomas shouted back, we will not agree about that night in Poros either. You will not like my script.

The drilling stopped for a few seconds.

So what happened, do you think?

It's not worth the scrutiny. I wanted to screw you, he shouted to everyone in the restaurant, but you didn't want the same thing.

The drilling started again.

Well, I agree, I was practically screaming now, but you can say 'She didn't want to screw me' in your own voice and not mine.

He'd cut his hair shorter and was wearing a suit.

The oysters were carried to the table on a stainless-steel tray loaded with crushed ice. Apparently, the urchins were finished. Someone else had ordered six of them before we did. Tomas suggested I put on my bikini, grab a fork and go hunt them down.

You are brutal, he said.

Maybe I am.

The waiter poured us each a glass of the Muscadet. To taste that first oyster on my tongue in Bastille was like being returned to the ocean. The dust of the Métro still on my clothes, in my hair, the traffic and sirens still in my head, Paris on the soles of my shoes. Tomas leaned forwards and tapped my nose with his finger, which was cold from the ice.

Actually, your own voice is quite weird. I mean your accent. Your English accent. I can't place it.

I was born in Ipswich, I heard myself tell him. I lived there for the first six years of my life.

How's it going in Paris anyway? he asked, as if I had said something unimportant. Are you still reading about Isadora Duncan?

Yes. She was often hungry in her childhood. Her mother knitted gloves and hats so Isadora could sell them door to door. Sometimes they had no money to find lodgings for the night.

Why are you so interested?

I think my own mother must have been poor.

You don't know for sure?

I do know.

The drilling began again. The time and space between the stopping and starting was very charged. Ten seconds, three seconds, a minute. It reminded me of the tractor stranded in the field near Ipswich, its engine also starting and stopping. My hand rested on the crushed ice on which the oysters were perched. When I said, 'I do know,' I glimpsed again in Paris what had come to me in London St Pancras. The piano, the Bösendorfer grand, being pulled by the tractor to the house of my foster-parents. But something new was happening. Something incredible. The men separated the tractor from the trailer. There was shouting. And then silence. A farmer led two horses into the field. It was the horses who pulled the trailer across the field towards my childhood house. At the same time, Tomas was talking, his lips were moving, the waiter hovered nearby, our wine glasses were empty and now Tomas was looking at something in the distance, as one would look at the horizon to halt seasickness.

My piano had arrived.

It was a serious piano.

It was funny, Tomas said, that we didn't make love on a beach called Love Bay.

If love could speak, how would she sound? The Bösendorfer grand had arrived at the house. I touched it and it touched me back. I thought of it as my mother's body. We would never be separated from each other again.

Searching for her in the piano.
Searching for her in the hat.

Tomas suggested we go elsewhere for coffee. And then he would have to get back to his film on Proust's bedroom. He wanted to know if I had read *Remembrance of Things Past*. Depending on the translation, it was sometimes titled *In Search of Lost Time*.

Searching everywhere. Every day.

19

Every day I made the journey to the Joséphine Baker pool on the edge of the Seine. It was built on a barge. I could swim on the Seine without actually being in it. For the time being I was a horizontal swimmer. I was convinced the woman who had bought the horses was thinking about me. It was urgent I found her. These were my precious last two days in Paris before I returned to London. I walked for hours alone in the Luxembourg Gardens searching for her. She had the horses that had pulled my mother's body closer to me. What use were they to her?

I thought I saw her standing by the ATM at the bank on Boulevard Raspail. She had her back to me, tall and lean in tight black trousers, a tight red chiffon blouse tucked into the waistband. She made her way to Café Select across the road, so I followed her. She was reading a newspaper. A man walked up to her table and kissed her on the lips. Then he sat down and she kissed him on the lips. Then she pulled him closer to her and kissed him again. It did not seem likely to me that my double sunbathed on the shores of love. The woman in Le Select was not on the shore so much as in the deep end.

Maybe I will be.

Maybe you will be what?

Forever.

Forever what?

I did not always have to answer the woman who had bought the horses.

The night before, I'd had a dream that she and I were going to have to swim to an island. We would make the journey at night. I suggested to her that we charter a boat, but she preferred to do the swim. In fact we were excited about the swim, it felt like we could do it, we were capable of this journey. While we were mentally preparing ourselves for the long voyage out, she was trying on fashionable white shoes with thick chunky soles and gold buckles. I understood then that we had more or less agreed to swim from somewhere safe (home) to somewhere unknown (the island), but we were putting off the moment to leave because she was trying on shoes. These white shoes were not the kind of shoes she would usually choose to wear, but I was telling her she looked good in them. I wondered if I had paused the risky journey we needed to make by introducing the white shoes to slow down the moment we would set off.

The concierge had left me a message about the keys to the Saint-Germain apartment. I was to return them to her at precisely 2.30 this afternoon. I had now packed up my clothes and books and checked the seat number on the Eurostar. It was still only eleven in the morning, so I walked across the road to have a coffee at the café by Maubert-Mutualité Métro station.

From my table on the terrace I looked out at the cheese shop across the road, the wine shop, the butcher and the five taxis parked in a line at the rank. Chalked on a blackboard at this café was the information there would be happy hour from 5pm to 8pm. The waiters were still masked, even for the happy hours, white strings looped over their ears.

After a while, a homeless man asked me for some money. At that moment the winter sun lit my little table on the terrace. Its rays warmed my face and when my fingers, now sunlit, fumbled in my purse, I discovered I had no loose change. I gave him the fifty-euro note I had zipped up with my London door keys. The odd thing, especially after the dream the night before, was that a damp swimming costume was also in my bag. He wanted me to give it to him. He was gesturing to me to hand over the shabby costume with its criss-crossed straps. His desire for it was intense.

I thought he might even cry when I refused to give it to him. At the same time, I was tormented with the regret of not swimming out to the island with my double in the dream. O broken world, you have captured my mind. I did not invest in that swim towards love.

After he left, now holding my damp swimming costume, I was for a few minutes basking, maybe even bathing, in this golden November sunshine.

I was grateful for its momentary warmth because my coat was at the dry-cleaners on Rue des Carmes. When I looked at the white ticket it said it would be ready on Saturday. Today was Tuesday and I was leaving for London. So now I had no coat in Paris in November and no swimming costume.

The waiter was saying something to me.

Madame, if he asked for your shoes would you give them to him?

If he asked for your hat, would you give it to him? Is he your cousin?

The sun had now moved on, as it must, as we all must move on, which is what I thought the dream was trying to convey to me. A small yellow car stopped at the traffic lights. Standing in the back were four llamas. I checked to see if this could be true. The red lights took a long time to change and it was true. All their heads were pointing in the same direction. That is to say, they were looking to the right, so I looked to the right. They were gazing at the light bulbs strung around the scaffolding of the market stalls at Place Maubert. How serene it is, I thought, to sit still for a while, in one place. It's possible that a yellow car will pass by with four llamas standing in the back.

And it's certain that someone poor will ask you for money.

The llamas were like a soft, calming pause from the horses that had pulled the piano across the field to my childhood home. I knew I would return to Paris to find my double and to claim my coat from the dry-cleaners.

20

LONDON, DECEMBER

Rajesh moved in with me for the Christmas season.

He had recently bought a kitten and named her Lucy. He said he wanted a calming name because he was convinced we would all be extinct soon. We were living in end times, as far as he was concerned. Inflation would rise, sea levels would rise, everybody would be out of work and underwater. The kitten moved in too. I liked to watch her soft paws walk across the keys of my Steinway, which Rajesh had uncovered and sometimes played to try and lure me to it. She was black with a white belly and skipped joyfully around the flat all day and night. We set up a litter tray in the bathroom. For some reason, every time we played chess, Lucy left the front room and made her way to the bathroom. The way she organized her toilet rituals delighted Rajesh.

We know too much about each other's personal habits, he murmured, scooping up his cat and kissing her ears. We're about to play chess, Lucy. Isn't it time to shit?

In the evenings when we played chess, the knight reminded me of the llamas I had seen in that yellow car in Paris. While I wrangled with Rajesh's chaotic mind on the chessboard – what was he doing with his queen? – I told him about Aimée's Siamese.

I think the family doctor attempted to molest her. That's the impression she gave me. The cat was her double, it saw him off. Rajesh's eyes filled with tears. His eyelashes were long and silky.

Don't you have more calming stories?

No.

I was serene when I was a teenager, he said. I became neurotic at twenty when I started to drink avocado smoothies and tried to only think positive thoughts.

My neighbour Gaby, short for Gabriella, came over with some takeaway fried chicken. Gaby wanted to know about my new lover. What new lover? Well, you're wearing his hat. No, I said. It's not his hat. It's her hat. And by the way, Rajesh is just a friend.

It was as if I was keeping the hat hostage in North London. It slept on a hook on the back of the living-room door. It was not a calm presence, more like a question floating through time, which in London was one hour behind Paris, two hours behind Athens.

I had forgotten to tell Aimée that Erik Satie thought it was bad manners to ask the point to a question.

Gaby opened the box of fried chicken and passed me a plastic fork. There had recently been a scandal in a British seaside town. A woman had found three small feathers in her fried chicken. At first she thought they were tiny legs. She plucked out the feathers and there was a photo in the newspaper of them lying in the palm of her hand. The manager had apparently explained that this was not up to the usual high standards of the fast fry, but the feathers were harmless. Rajesh thought it was a good thing to bring the animal home, the equivalent of finding a pig's tooth in your sausage. He opened all the windows while Gaby and I ate the chicken, as if somehow the bird could now fly away.

When Gaby left, we lay on the floor and listened to Ravi Shankar's *Morning Raga*. It was midnight. The kitten played with a bauble on the tree. Our presents were wrapped and placed under the twinkling fairy lights we had threaded between its branches. It was as if we were waiting for something, but it wasn't Christmas Day.

Rajesh persuaded me to rehearse a duet for piano and clarinet to play for Arthur. Every time we played together there was something like the idea of an erotic charge in the room. We both knew it and tried to ignore it, but it was there, like the first winter snow that had fallen on the muddy shore of the Thames. We had gone mudlarking at low tide. To my surprise, Rajesh revealed he often spent his weekends on the foreshore close to Southwark Bridge. We had found the bowl and broken stem of an ornate clay pipe. Rajesh thought it was from the eighteenth century, when every village would have had its own clay-pipe maker.

It was when he played the clarinet that his beauty was in full flower, even in the winter snow, his breath long and deep, the way he wet the cane with his spit before attaching it to the mouthpiece.

During one of our rehearsals, Marcus FaceTimed me. They were writing music now and had enjoyed the task of composing something that lasted two minutes and twelve seconds for the cello. Working with Bella had changed life for the better.

I did not know how to begin to tell Bella I was spending so much time with Rajesh. For this reason, I had not answered her various texts, which were all about her lessons with Marcus.

In fact, I was so keen to get off the subject

of Bella, I told Marcus about Isadora Duncan setting up a dance school in Germany. She had at last earned some money from her international performances. It was such a relief, I said, to think that Isadora, who had often gone to bed hungry as a child, now had lots of loot. She bought a villa in Berlin and went shopping for furniture at the Wertheim department store.

What did she buy?

I could hear Marcus yawning on the island of Poros.

She bought forty little beds for her students. And she placed a statue of a mythic female warrior in the main hall of the villa. She wanted to make a paradise for the children. None of them would be hungry. They all ate a vegetarian diet and danced to Beethoven and Brahms and to Chopin's 'Funeral March'.

Yeah, Marcus said, were they orphans?

I don't know.

Maybe I am.

Maybe you are what?

*

Marcus told me their brother's boarding school in Britain was nothing like Isadora's school. In fact it was the opposite, from what they could tell. Not upwards and outwards. No skipping and bending.

Perhaps they should all do The Isadora instead of rugby? Can you start a war while skipping around in a flimsy toga?

Rajesh interrupted to point out that the toga-wearing ancient Greeks were always at war.

My father is also always at war, Marcus said, and he wears a long ponytail and sneakers. My mother is always at war too, mostly with my father, and she wears diamond earrings.

Maybe I was.

Maybe you were what?

An orphan.

After that call, I went off alone to buy two toma-tillos at the new rip-off organic grocery shop. It was a fruit, red like menstrual blood, sweet and fleshy.

21

I first tasted a tomatillo with Arthur in Colombia when I was thirty. We were staying for two days in Cartagena after a concert in Bogotá. The juicy tomatillo was the only fruit that Arthur would eat in Colombia. He was convinced the 'uncooked fish', which is what he called the ceviche served everywhere, would kill him. He mostly existed on cheese-flavoured crisps until we discovered the hotel staff served a tomatillo for breakfast every morning. Shaped like a large egg, its taste was sweet and sour, invigorating, maybe similar to a passion fruit. On the morning we discovered the tomatillo, a dark blue bird with golden eyes and a long tail landed on our table and positioned itself near the bread basket. Its left golden eye began to swell and expand, as if it were going to pop out of its head, and then it suddenly made off with our bread in its beak. It was as if we could literally see the planning of the bread heist in its left eye.

Yes, Arthur said, when we are possessed with inspiration, like this bird, the body alters, it changes.

I was possessed with inspiration. As soon as I arrived home, I opened up the tomatillos, scooped out the black seeds and planted them in a black plastic tray. Every day I watered them, and waited. A blade of grass pushed up a week later. The grass quivered if I touched it. As the seedlings came up, I began to think of the single blade as a mother, or mistress of ceremonies. This single blade of grass was introducing the young seedlings to each other. It was growing taller and it now had three blades. The blades curved to reach over the newer seedlings. They were definitely talking to each other.

The seedlings smelled of midnight and hot stones in the rain.

Like her.

22

On Christmas Day, Rajesh and I played George Gershwin's 'Rhapsody in Blue' for Arthur. We placed my phone on a music stand and began the concert on FaceTime. Rajesh gave it his all, long breaths, bending his knees, rising to the tip of his toes. Arthur sat in an armchair, wrapped in a red velvet shawl. A book lay on his lap. He looked thin and fragile. At times he closed his eyes, as if this, too, was something he had to endure. His neighbour, Andrew, sat near him, now and again tucking Arthur's shawl under his shins.

Rajesh, you have become so plump, Arthur whispered.

That is all he had to say about the concert.

When Rajesh disappeared into the kitchen to make us tamarind fish, I left the phone on the music stand and followed him. My God, how I hate the midget king, he whispered. Do you think I've got plump? I shook my head and told him Arthur was demented, probably hallucinating. Rajesh started to furiously pestle ginger and garlic.

I returned to Arthur on the screen. He had opened the book on his lap. Not to be outdone by our performance, he declared he wanted to recite his favourite words by Walt Whitman.

I knew them off by heart anyway. He had read them to me since I was twelve.

. . . dismiss whatever insults your own soul;
and your very flesh shall be a great poem,
and have the richest fluency, not only in its
words, but in the silent lines of its lips and
face, and between the lashes of your eyes,
and in every motion and joint of your body.

Rajesh was now shouting from the kitchen. Something about his soul being insulted by Arthur and how much he loathed him in every joint of his body and between the hairs under his arms and between the silence of every goose-bump on his balls.

Andrew's face appeared on the screen. He was gaunt, with icy-blue eyes. Apparently, they were going to leave now to have their Christmas lunch with the pharmacist and his wife.

I asked him to give the phone back to Arthur.

Elsa, Arthur said, where are you?

I'm in London.

Still blue?

Arthur, let me show you the tomatillo seedlings I have grown for you.

I carried my phone towards the trays that now lined the windowsill and pointed the camera at the heart-shaped leaves, fragile and perfect.

My dear, he said, we will meet under its fruit-laden boughs when the pandemic is over.

Arthur, I replied, I think you knew my mother.

Andrew's face appeared on the screen.

Maestro is tired, knock it off.

Was she your student?

Who?

My mother.

This was the conversation that he had dreaded ever since he adopted me.

You will have to read the documents.

The fairy lights twinkled on the tree that Rajesh and I had decorated together. Chocolate liqueurs hung from the boughs. The kitten dabbed at one of them and then pulled it off. This was the most homely Christmas I had ever had in my life. It was as if we were living inside one of the pictures on the advent calendars that are stocked in the shops from October. Rajesh celebrated Diwali more than he celebrated Christmas. He had made it all for me.

Show me the tomatillos again, Arthur wheezed.

I swerved the phone back to the windowsill.

Ah, Arthur intoned, just as Walt Whitman inseminated American poetry with the long-cadenced line, the tomatillo seeds have inseminated me and now I am an orchard.

Rajesh walked moodily around the flat in shorts and leather sandals while the fish cooked. He did not seem to feel the cold. Perhaps he was still stung by Arthur's comment. I made us both a Christmas negroni while he shaved in the bathroom, watched by Lucy in her litter tray. He always listened to John Cage's *Piano Works* in the mornings.

I heard your conversation with Arthur, he said over lunch.

With a spoon and knife he expertly removed the succulent white flesh from the sea bream. It had a long spine. That morning he had woken an hour earlier than usual to soak the tamarind in boiling water before he smashed it to a pulp.

Why do you think he knew your birth mother?

Well, Rajesh, how did he know about me?

What do you mean?

He arrived at the house in Ipswich and asked the child prodigy to play for him.

I don't understand.

Someone told him about me.

You must have thought about this before.

Forever. Never. Maybe.

Rajesh stripped what was left of the fish off the bone and ladled more coconut rice on to his plate. After a while, he said, I am not listening to what you mean. I'm just listening to your words as sounds.

I changed the subject and told him about Tomas instead. He wanted to know how we had said goodbye at the brasserie in Bastille. Did we go back to his bedroom to continue talking about Proust's bedroom?

I was too busy slipping slivers of sea bream to his kitten to bother telling him what had happened next. When his mother rang from Dublin, they talked for a while on speakerphone. She must have forgotten I was sitting opposite him, because she asked why he was living with the blue freak.

Rajesh hysterically threw his phone on the floor.

Oh my God, he moaned, slapping his hands over his eyes.

I just heard her words as traffic sounds on a busy road, I reassured him.

I'll do the Isadora, he suddenly shouted at Lucy.

He moved a few chairs out of the way, kicked off his sandals, opened his arms wide, lifted his chest, grabbed the fish spine from the plate, held it aloft in his right hand, twirled, skipped, leaped, fell to the floor, rose again, jumped on to the sofa where I was sitting and gently, fiercely, slowly, kissed me on the lips. We had sex for the rest of the afternoon while the kitten frolicked by our ankles.

A choir of six residents from the lower-ground floor began to sing carols in the car park. John Cage was still playing on Rajesh's music system in the bathroom. Lucy had fallen asleep on my piano.

If only Tomas knew, Rajesh said afterwards.

Knew what?

The way to get closer to the green jewel in your belly button is to dance with a fish bone.

Marie called to wish us both a happy Christmas. She had lost her taste for confusion and uncertainty and was spending the big day writing her next book. She had told Julia to leave, but she was still in love with her. Julia had three other lovers and Marie thought that was three too many. Rajesh reckoned that if she'd lost her taste for confusion and uncertainty, she would be alone for the holidays next year, as well.

23

I cycled to the Serpentine two days after Boxing Day. The snow had melted and London was deserted. As I walked my bike through Hyde Park, I saw a Rastafarian man standing under a tree with a green parakeet perched on his shoulder. He was holding up an apple and the bird was pecking at it. Every now and again he changed the pitch of his whistle, low to high, high to low, rolling the *rrr*'s to lure them to him. Another parakeet flew from the tree to land on his shoulder. I watched him and the parakeets for a long time. It was interesting listening to the sounds he made to call the birds and the way they called back to him. After a while, he walked towards a particular bush, still with the birds balanced on his shoulder, and picked a single sprig of some sort of berry. Suddenly someone was shouting at him.

Can you read English?

A man, about sixty, walking his dog on the path, was pointing to a sign fixed to the railings.

It says in English picking flowers in the park is forbidden.

It didn't have to be so ridiculous, one man picking a sprig of berries, another man harassing him, but it was how it was. I pointed to the dog who had now run off the path and was frantically digging up the grass.

Can you see to your dog?

Fuck off, you ugly bitch.

He was white, angry and flabby, and the Bird Whistler was the opposite, brown, toned, gentle. It just happened to be how it was. You can't get parakeets to come to you if you're aggressive. The Bird Whistler ignored us both and walked away, light on his feet. The white man's head was so infected with anger and self-pity it made his eyes stupid and small. It didn't have to be like that, he could have been educated and handsome and still stupid, but it happened to be how it was.

Listen, he said, and then he listed the whole composition, almost word-perfect: slut, dyke, mental. He left out *hag* but made up for it by adding some extra insulting words about the Rastafarian, nothing new, always the same old. After all, he'd actually asked me to listen to his composition, ending with: You shouldn't be riding your bicycle in the park.

I'm not riding it, I'm walking it, I shouted back. Which was true. When he waddled towards me, swinging his dog lead like a whip, I asked myself: What would Marie do? I swung my leg over my bike and cycled fast towards him until he had to jump off the path and get out of my way. It was always the same people making the same old.

There was a hole in the concrete path and I was toppled off my bike before I made it to the gates. Later, I smothered my bruised left thigh with salve of arnica.

Arnica, the flower, is related to the sunflowers of my childhood.

Blazing in the field above the forbidden

pasture. The pasture made me feel anxious, excited, forlorn. I wrote my score in fragments through the winter and into the spring. It was full of dissonant harmonic intervals. I was never far from the piano, but I heard my composition in my head anyway. Sometimes I had to write it down to hear it, and, more mysteriously, before I could hear it. When Rajesh moved out, we agreed we were better suited as friends. He knew the humiliation of Vienna had begun to lose its power over me. I knew he was recovering from a broken marriage and the lockdown happening at the same time. He was a very skilled and collaborative musician. He needed work. It did feel like end times when he called to say his kitten was sick. The vet could find nothing wrong with her. There was a week when she yowled through the day and he could no longer be in the same room as her. And then she stopped yowling, at times she even purred, but what he heard in his head were the sounds he had tried not to listen to. All the same, he was comforted by the low rumbling of her occasional happiness.

I was out of work too, living on my savings

and royalties from recordings. There were weeks when I played fragments of my score through the night, which is when I felt most in communion with the woman who had bought the horses. I projected myself into her and she became music. The air was electric between us as we transmitted our feelings to each other across three countries. When she emerged from the shadows of my imagination into minims and quavers, it was almost like being in love. It was a sublime and sometimes shocking transmission, but not as shocking as the message transmitted to me by Andrew when he phoned me from Sardinia. He told me that Arthur had been diagnosed with a tumour on the lung. The prognosis was anything from three weeks to two months.

Elsa, he said, his voice tight and hard, I suppose that for an exotic bird like yourself, putting ointment on Arthur's bedsores will be a bit of a comedown?

24

SARDINIA, JULY

I flew to Cagliari on a Dutch airline. My father is very ill, I said to the cabin staff, to be honest he is dying. It was the first time I had ever called Arthur my father and meant it. They were kind. Various crew members came to my seat to ask if I was okay. It's not a question that can be easily answered with a yes or a no. The airline meal arrived with a tiny pair of orange plastic clogs filled with salt and pepper.

I was seated at the back of the aircraft. The cabin crew made arrangements for me to be the first to exit the plane. My fear was that Arthur might die before I arrived.

*

Andrew had arranged for the man who ran the newsagent in the town where he and Arthur lived to pick me up from the airport. The agreed price was sixty euro. At ten at night it was still humid and windless. I was dripping with sweat before I even clambered into the old car. When Rajesh called, I asked him to water my tomatillo plants. He wished me courage. I didn't know what to say back.

In a way, courage was my problem.

Not lack of it.

The way courage silenced everything else.

Andrew was waiting for me. A lamp post on the pavement projected a spectral light on to two humble houses that were built side by side. He was about sixty and had grown a full beard since I last saw him on FaceTime. It was threaded with silver and made him seem kinder than he was in life. He had been watering the bougainvillea that grew up the wall between the two houses, and held a hosepipe in his hand. Neither friendly nor unfriendly, he was clearly king of the domain between his house and Arthur's. A television blared at high volume in the empty bar across the road from the two houses.

Buona sera.

An elderly woman walking her poodle stopped to greet Andrew. Her dog had black curly hair and she had white curly hair. Andrew started to talk to her in Italian while he coiled the hosepipe around a hook on the wall. I asked him to take me to Arthur.

Well now, Elsa, you're suddenly in a hurry to visit the sick old man?

The woman stared directly at me as I stood there with my suitcase, sweating under the lamp post.

So, she's arrived, she said to Andrew.

He wore leather sandals and jeans. In a way he was quite youthful and energetic.

When I take you into Arthur's house, he said, you will need to wash your hands and wear a mask because of the travelling. The Maestro is weak, so we must not tire him. The way he said *Maestro*. The Master. As if Arthur belonged to him. He pointed to a marble sink on the porch outside Arthur's house. I washed my hands using what was left of an old slab of soap.

Arthur was lying in bed. He was emaciated and tiny but his eyes were bright. The living room had been made into a bedroom. A cranky old fan on the ceiling whirled its blades above his head.

Elsa, where are you?

I'm in Sardinia.

But where are you?

I'm here with you.

Still blue, he said.

My face was masked. He did not wear a mask because it hindered his breathing. I reached for his hand. Andrew was also unmasked. He lifted Arthur to sitting position, which meant we had to untangle our fingers while he held a glass of water to Arthur's dry and blistered lips. There was something hostile in the way he parted our hands.

Thank you, angel, Arthur whispered.

I wasn't sure who he was talking to.

*

It was a shock to see the tall Victorian lamp from England standing beside his bed. It had a dusty, pink-fringed shade. I had grown up with that lamp in the house in Richmond. Also the kilim rug with the scorpion woven into its centre. Placed on it was the furniture of my childhood, the brown velvet armchair with its matching footstool. Most shocking of all was Arthur's Steinway pushed against the wall in the corner of the room. This was the piano on which Arthur had taught his students. How had he managed to get it here? I knew every centimetre of this tormentor intimately. When I was eight, Arthur spent three hours every day teaching me how to use my thumbs when I played fast octaves. His title for the lesson was 'Passage of the Curved Resentful Thumbs'.

A thin layer of dust had settled on the lid, which was closed. I had never seen it closed. There was always someone playing that piano, or tuning it, or swearing at it, or polishing it. I knew the keys were made from ivory, long outlawed. It was an old piano. The keys were more yellow than white. Ivory doesn't burn. Arthur had told me that in the old days, he taught composers who played with one hand and smoked with the other. When ash dropped on the keys they would have melted if they had been made from plastic. It was a beast of a piano. Some of it was made from elephants. In this dark room, in this modest house, one of the most famous pianos in the world had been pushed against the thick stone wall. It was famous because Arthur's students were famous. A pile of dead flies lay on its maple lid.

Elsa will need some help opening the window of her room, Arthur told Andrew.

All fingers and thumbs then, Andrew replied.

I was not sure what he meant.

Stay with me a little, Arthur whispered in his new small voice. Don't fly away. We are where we are.

We are where we are, I repeated.

And where are you, Elsa?

Perhaps there was no one in the world who better understood me. And misunderstood me. His main task when I was a child was to focus my wandering attention. His question went back a long way.

Now I heard it as a refrain, a repeated musical phrase.

I'm here with you, I replied.

My words were muffled under the mask.

It began to dawn on me, at that moment, that I was going to lose him. It didn't matter if I wore a mask.

Andrew showed me to my room. He told me that Arthur could no longer walk and would need some help at night to get to the bathroom. The room was dark, with a small window and a single bed covered in a white lace bedspread. Andrew seemed keen to leave and wished me goodnight. Next to the bed was a small walnut table with curved legs. Something was resting on top of it. I already knew what it was he had put there. The documents, the adoption papers. All the same, it was a shock. Perhaps a violation. I had not asked for them, after all. I picked up the grey folder and slid it under the mattress of my chaste single bed. I wanted to know the bus routes in this town more than I wanted to read the adoption papers. A rage as old as the elephant that had died to become a piano entered my body.

It's there anyway.

What is there anyway?

It hasn't just entered your body.

What hasn't?

I was hungry and thirsty but did not dare leave my room. I could hear Andrew in the kitchen. Why did he not leave Arthur's house and return to his own? He seemed to be frying onions. He had not even offered me a glass of water, only instructed me to wash my hands. Flies circled the light bulb hanging from the ceiling. I could hear the loud television in the bar and feral cats fighting in the street outside. I took off my shoes and lay down on the bed.

When I woke up three hours later, Andrew was calling me.

I ran into the living room in a panic. He

wanted to show me how to lift Arthur so we could walk him to the toilet. Maestro was to stretch out his arms in front of him like a zombie, and we would place our arms under his left and right armpit to lift him up. For the first time I understood that calling him Maestro was Andrew's way of giving a dying man some status. Did Arthur appreciate it? He was so small and thin we could have carried him to the bathroom. It seemed that Andrew wanted to give him the dignity of walking there himself. The heat was still intense. We were all dripping with sweat at two in the morning. I was awake for the rest of the night. When I tiptoed into the kitchen to find a bottle of water, I saw that Arthur was lying in Andrew's arms. They lay in bed together, the creaking blades whirring above them. The other sound was Arthur's breathing.

har har har har har har

It was almost inaudible, but it filled the room.

25

Still here?

Yes.

Elsa, you are a miracle.

Arthur reached for my hand in the bright morning light.

Andrew was there too, seething behind his beard.

Is it time for a piss, Maestro?

No. Please. My egg.

Andrew brought in a tray with Arthur's breakfast.

Egg, toast, tea. He tapped the egg and started to feed Arthur, who said his eyes hurt because his eyelashes were growing inwards.

I consider you family, he said.

Yellow yolk ran down his chin.

I thought, Yes, well, you are almost my father. Why wouldn't we be family? And then I realized he meant his neighbour as well.

I carried the tray back to the kitchen and washed up the dishes. Andrew explained that if I wanted breakfast there was a small supermarket in town where I could buy bread and coffee and water.

Whatever I wanted I should provide for myself.

Arthur, I said, when I walked back into the living room, I'm off to the shops. Do you want anything?

I'd like a sausage roll.

There are no sausage rolls as Maestro understands them in Sardinia, Andrew interrupted.

I will try and find Mr Goldstein a sausage roll as he understands it, I replied.

Arthur parted his lips and made a strange hissing sound. I realized he was laughing.

Bells were ringing somewhere in the town.

I glanced at the row of framed photographs propped up on the bookshelves. They were all of a younger Arthur and Andrew. Both of them tanned, smiling, holding flowers and vegetables from the market, or sitting in a restaurant, Andrew's arm around Arthur's left shoulder. The last one was taken on a train. Arthur wore a white linen suit and a red cravat. He seemed to be in animated conversation with Andrew, who, gaunt and smiling, was holding up a glass jar of green olives for the camera. Perhaps he was forty and Arthur sixty in these photographs. I finally understood they had long been lovers. Love with a moron was more possible in the south.

They looked happy and peaceful with each other.

I walked into the deserted town and found a café in the square, opposite the church. Apart from the waiters, the few people in town seemed old. Maybe the children were all at school, because there were two small bicycles leaning against the wall of a house. As I sipped my coffee, I suddenly felt young, tragic, maybe even evil. I wanted Andrew to die instead of Arthur. I wished I had seduced Tomas in Paris. What if

I took off all my clothes and ran naked through the town to look for a sausage roll? I began to sing fragments of the music I had been composing in London. This time I added to it the sound of Arthur's breath from the night before.

har har har har har har

My audience were the two feral cats who sat by my feet. They had obviously spent their life fighting in the streets of this town. I lowered my head in their direction and, very softly, watched by their golden eyes, sang to them in the early morning sun:

Elsa, where are you?

I am here with you.

har har har har har

One of them had no ears at all. The tabby had one remaining stump. I took a photograph of the cats and sent it to Aimée with a message:

My students in Sardinia. One ear between them.

There were no sausage rolls as Arthur would understand them in the local bakery. I found the gelateria instead and walked in to buy ice cream. While I stared in a daze at the freezer, Rajesh called to ask how it was going. I read out the flavours to him in Green Lanes, London: Pistacchio, cioccolato, stracciatella, mandorla.

We agreed that for Arthur there were only two flavours: chocolate and vanilla. I think Andrew wants to murder me, I whispered to my oldest friend. He won't let me spend any time alone with Arthur.

I did not mention my own murderous thoughts.

And then I told him that our teacher was going to slip away.

But how are you, Elsa?

I'm like this, I said, and began to sing into the phone:

Elsa, where are you?
I am here with you.
har har har har har

I think you should add strawberry flavour, fragola, to the mix, Rajesh finally replied.

And then he sang to me:
Mandorla, fragola, stracciatella.

On the way back to the dark, dusty house, the woman who had been walking the poodle passed me and waved cheerfully in my direction. When she saw my tears, she crossed herself. The ice cream was already melting in my hands.

Elsa, you are here.

Yes.

Arthur wanted to try the chocolate ice cream straight away.

Andrew fed him with a spoon.

No, angel, he said to Andrew. You must keep the spoon longer in my mouth so that I can relish it.

That's what it comes down to in the end days. A little ice cream on a teaspoon is everything. His mind was wandering. He said everything on his mind without cancelling his thoughts.

I made you who you are.

And I made you who you are, I replied.

Andrew laughed and started to spoon the ice cream into his own mouth.

Arthur lifted his hands as if to control the traffic.

The gesture he made to Andrew was *Stop*.

I hope it will rain soon and we can get some sleep.

He turned his head towards me.

The child Elsa has many faces. I have studied them all.

I'm sure the Lord will make it rain only for Elsa, Andrew intoned in the style of a sombre priest. Arthur placed a thin finger on his lips.

Hush, he whispered, the concert is about to begin.

If I had been wearing a pair of Greek slippers, I would have reached for the dagger hidden in the pompom and plunged it into Andrew's scabby thigh.

That night we lifted Arthur out of bed and walked him to the bathroom five times. At three in the morning the lights went out. Something to do with a generator. Andrew told me there was a light bulb I could buy and charge on my computer for ten hours. Then I could screw it into a light fitting and it would come on during the blackouts. So why hadn't he bought it?

We need a night nurse, I suggested nervously.

Andrew agreed it could be arranged if I wanted to give the agency my credit-card details. He was tired and insisted we needed a day nurse as well. With his help I managed to book two nurses for the following week. In the meantime, I sliced oranges and took them to Arthur, who had more or less stopped eating. There were melons growing in his sandy garden. Most of the grapes had shrivelled on the vines. Arthur told me the melons were too bright. I'm over all that, he said. What did he mean? There is too much life in a melon, he murmured, as if that explained everything. I sat on a chair by his side with ice wrapped in a tea towel, holding it to his forehead. He wasn't in the mood for talking. I began to chain-smoke on the porch while my teacher was dying of a lung tumour. The gold lighter I had found in Poros, engraved with the word *Champ*, had travelled with me from Love Bay to Sardinia. Love and Death, entwined.

26

I met my mother in a dream.

She was playing the piano and I was lying under the piano. I watched her feet on the pedals, felt the vibrations from the wood enter my ribs. I will kiss you twelve times behind your ear before I go, she said. Suddenly we were in a car and a baby was sitting next to me. It licked my fingers with its warm pink tongue. I said to my mother, Do you have a bottle? Meaning a bottle of milk for the baby, but she didn't have one. The mother was empty, or emptied out. Hollow but there.

I realized I did not know what my mother looked like. The same could be said for my double. I had gazed at her, chased after her, but I did not have a sharp visual memory of her face.

*

Arthur reached out and grasped my hand.

Elsa, there is music in your hand. Flowing into my hand.

He did not let go.

I have the documents for you here.

I told him that if I read the adoption documents the music would already be written and I would have nothing to write about.

Write about what? Rachmaninov is Rachmaninov.

He encouraged me to drink a glass of cola. We were regressing to our early years together, when I was ten.

Arthur, can you hear me?

Yes.

Was my mother your student. In the past?

He stared at the wall.

She told you about me, when I was six?

I have left the house in Richmond to you and the Italian house to Andrew, he replied.

Spit dribbled down his chin. Flies circled his head.

Read the documents, Elsa.

It will be the same old story, I said.

Why not let her be? he replied. Let her find the moon.

It was like pressing on a bruise. To be so helplessly chained to this old story. Written by the officials who were obliged to record it in the documents. To be forced to read the words they wrote for every abandoned child.

Mandorla, fragola, stracciatella.
They were more interesting words.

Maybe they are not?
Maybe they are not what?
More interesting words.
Her voice inside me. Like a handful of small stones thrown at a window.

I told Andrew about my conversation with Arthur while he peeled potatoes on the porch. He poured water from a jug into two glasses and handed one of them to me. He drained his glass. It seemed to revive his hostility.

You are very cruel not to have read the documents, he said.

Arthur has had to carry the burden of what's inside them for decades. Your preference for ignorance has cost him.

I bent down to buckle my sandal so as not to look at his eyes. The stitching around the buckle had come loose. It was going to fall off. While I fiddled with the buckle, it reminded me of the bronze statue of Montaigne on the Rue des Écoles in Paris, how I touched his shiny shoe on the way to teach Aimée.

I had looked up Montaigne. Something he had written came to mind while Andrew's knife made a circle of peel: 'Ignorance is the softest pillow on which a man can lay his head.' There was nowhere to lay my head that was as comforting as ignorance. What was the point of laying my head on something harsh, unbearable, like the documents? I had moved them from under the mattress and stuck them in the cupboard under a dusty blanket. Moving the story out of sight. Andrew had more to say in the half-shade of the porch. At one point he picked a grape from the vines growing above his head, threw it in the air and caught it in his open mouth. It was as if this was the cue for him to begin a long-rehearsed speech.

Arthur looked after you since you were a child and now he is eighty. But you asked no questions about how he was going to care for himself in old age.

He lifted his right arm and peered at the dry scaly patches on his elbow. It was called psoriasis, he said, not contagious, a dysfunction of the immune system. He could live with it. Arthur had lived with it too. They had spent many years embracing each other under the healing southern sun. Now, seeing there was a nurse arriving in an hour, he would drive me to the beach. He could do with a break himself, had I thought of that?

He picked another grape from the vines and this time crushed it between his fingers.

I had given my credit-card details to the agency. It seemed that Andrew had no funds of his own and was loath to ask Arthur for money. They had never married, he sighed, but in a sense, he supposed he was a kind of stepfather to me. After all – he lifted his head upwards to stare at the dying grapes – Arthur speaks of no one else and worries about no one else as much as he worries about you. And yet, he said directly, now wiping his lips with a rag of a handkerchief, it seems you have never asked him how he manages his everyday errands.

I was still fiddling with the buckle of my shoe.

It's hard to regard Arthur as a father.

I was whispering because I could hear Arthur breathing in the living room.

I was his child prodigy, but I was not his child.

Under the circumstances, Andrew replied, I think it's right that I should inherit the Richmond house.

No. It is my house. I am his child.

Make up your mind. He waved the knife near my lips, as if he wanted to cut out my tongue.

I returned to Arthur who was sleeping on his back. I sat on the edge of the bed and stared at the thick silver hair in his ears. After a while I sang to him:

Mandorla, fragola, stracciatella.
His chest lifted. His lips parted.
Mandorla, fragola, stracciatella.
He was singing back to me. I heard him.
When he raised his left hand, we touched fingertips.

Andrew told me to gather my swimming gear. He would put petrol in the car. He talked about petrol for quite a long time. As if it were a major operation. After a while it occurred to me that he was indirectly asking me to pay for it. I wondered how he earned his living. I had earned all my own money.

The nurse arrived and wanted to know about Arthur's medication. There was a certain pill he had to take after lunch every day. It was for pain relief and it was important that he ate something before he swallowed it. She was calm and kind. Her son was now eight months old, so she could only do day shifts. Her mother was looking after the child. Yesterday, she said, her mother had beheaded two chickens. She would cook them with tomatoes and olives for a family birthday. Maybe she would bring a portion for the sick man to eat before his pill.

My dear Eileen, Arthur wheezed, I hope your mother doesn't behead the child.

Her name was Francesca, but I knew who Eileen was. She was one of the au pairs who had looked after me when I was nine. I had shown her how to draw a treble clef while she sat on the brown velvet armchair that was now transplanted to Arthur's Italian life.

Like myself, it was now witness to his slow exit from life.

Andrew filled the car with petrol and I paid for it. He needed some time off from the caring. He repeated this refrain many times. It was his first break for a while. He was ragged with exhaustion. He hadn't slept a night through for weeks. I suggested he go to bed and catch up on sleep instead of driving to the beach. I would help Francesca.

And how will you help her?

She will tell me what to do.

No, Andrew said, we have petrol now.

It was as if he sensed I preferred her company to his own.

When I had opened the front door to let her into the house, something had happened. She had reached out to touch my blue hair. At the same time my fingers were touching the wings of the dragonfly brooch pinned to the collar of her blouse.

So you are the daughter, she whispered, bellissima, bellissima.

It seemed that Andrew was keen to separate me from Arthur and Francesca at all times. Yet he was also slyly suggesting that I had been neglectful of my teacher in his old age. It was as if I was in his debt and the Richmond house would repay a loan that I had never taken out in the first place.

A forest fire had blackened the trees on the road to the beach. The charred bark and boughs and bone-dry grass seemed to be the right mood for a day spent in the company of Andrew. We stopped for lunch at a small shack café by a reservoir between the road and beach. A man sat on a chair under an umbrella, scraping the scales off small silver fish. We ate spaghetti alle vongole in silence. The clams were sweet and salty. I licked the shells, suddenly ravenous. When I dipped the soft and smoky bread into the chilled red wine, Andrew told me I was eating too fast.

After that we stopped talking to each other.

Maybe I am.
  Maybe you are what?
  Greedy.

Andrew decided to break the silence and make small talk about life in the town. The woman working the tills in the supermarket was sleeping with someone's husband. The baker was indiscreet, best not to gossip with him. The yellow house where the priest lived, next to the church, had subsidence. The pharmacist, priest and mayor were the most important people in the town. You eat like a maniac, he said again, slow down, we are in the south.

*

Maybe I am.

Maybe you are what?

A maniac.

So, you have been living in Paris.

It was not exactly a question.

As it happens, he said, about six years ago, in early April, I was in Chablis, helping a friend who owns vineyards there.

He went on to tell me that when a severe frost had come to Chablis, they had filled cans with paraffin and lit them at night to keep the vines warm. The temperature plunged and many of the vines were damaged. The Romans apparently did this too. It was an ancient trick to warm the shivering vines. Did I know the Romans put cork on the soles of their shoes in winter? After water and milk, he said, wine was the main refreshment for ordinary Romans, but it was always mixed with water. To drink wine unmixed was considered barbaric. I interrupted him.

Where in Britain are you from?

Durham, originally.

I asked him if he worked and what had

brought him to Sardinia. He did not want to say anything more. I respected his wish and did not poke and prod and pummel. We finished the meal with espresso served in small white porcelain cups. On each saucer was a sachet of sugar made in Montichiari. Andrew gazed at me with his usual mocking expression.

I see you are interested in Montichiari, but you don't want to know about Ipswich.

Seems like you don't want to know about Durham either, I replied.

When the bill arrived, he waited for me to pay it. I took out the euro in my purse and paid for my share. It was the first time I fought back with Andrew. At the same time I was asking myself what Arthur saw in him. I couldn't understand why his life had become tangled with this person. He was a man who seemed to be lost. Damaged. How had he fetched up in this sweltering town and become the lover of my flamboyant teacher who could speak seven languages and read the Bible in Hebrew? Arthur had no time for what he called mediocrity. If you were plodding mediocrities, he would say to his students, I would not be teaching you. Yet it seemed that love was possible in the south with someone who called him Maestro.

The beach was a long stretch of sand dunes. White flowers grew between the stones and broken glass. Small flies crawled everywhere: in the sand, between my toes and fingers, on my lips. The lifeguard spent most of her time on her phone, now and again peering out at the open sea where people were diving into the waves. She said she lived in an apartment with some of the staff who worked at a local hotel in the summer. Six to a room. She pointed to a man in white robes walking the long stretch of the beach, selling rolls of cotton cloth. He wore nine straw hats piled on his head in a tower and was selling those too. Whenever someone seemed interested, he drew the price with his finger in the sand.

He's a farmer from Somalia, the lifeguard said. He knows how to grow olive trees, vegetables and strawberries. He walked across the desert of Sudan and Libya to get to Italy. She lifted her arm and waved at him. He turned around to face her and waved back, tall and elegant in his white robe, the wild green sea behind him.

I dived into the swelling waves and stayed in the sea for an hour to get away from Andrew. After a while the straps of my bikini top became loose. And then it came off. I had to swim with it in my hand, through the waves, towards the shore. When I was knee-deep, I attempted to tie it on again, my breasts exposed to everyone on the beach. Standing under the fierce sun, my half-naked body brought to me an apparition of my mother. Something I had seen, or perhaps summoned to comfort or torment myself, when I was six years old.

I tried to see her again as I fiddled with the straps, but the apparition dissolved in the light and churning froth. For some reason, in Sardinia, whenever I thought about my mother, she came straight to my fingers. I could write the notes in the sand, like the Somalian man who drew with his finger the price of the goods he was selling. When the waves crashed on the shore, the numbers disappeared without trace. Like her.

On the way home, I asked Andrew how we were going to keep Arthur cool. You're doing quite well with the ice, he replied, but he needs a modern air-conditioning system. I was sunburned from the time avoiding him in the sea. Out of the blue he asked me if I thought about my mother.

No, I said, I never think about her.

We drove home in silence through the charred and burned forest.

27

Play for me, Arthur whispered, play the Rach.

He pointed to his dusty Steinway in the corner.

I shook my head.

He wants to see his reflection in the river one last time, I heard my double whisper, close to my ear. You, Elsa M. Anderson, are his legend.

Maybe I am.

Maybe you are what?

Brutal.

Andrew showed me how to strip the skins off prickly pears. Their thin transparent spines were worse than the urchins'. The fruit was orange, full of seeds and juicy. Earlier in the year he had collected wild asparagus and frozen it. He did not share Arthur's basic tastes in food and cooked himself various meats with fennel flowers. We now ate breakfast together, only because we would then discuss our plan for Arthur's care for the day and I was doing all the shopping for groceries. Every day he boiled and mashed potatoes for Arthur.

After a while I stopped wearing sunblock. I slept in the hammock strung under the withered grapevines and turned brown straight away. The blue was growing out of my hair. I made friends with the woman who ran the embroidery school. Her name was Marielle. When she pierced cloth with her needle, she was an engineer possessed with inspiration.

The day nurse, Francesca, wanted to know how long I was staying.

Andrew translated her question, though he knew I understood it anyway, his brisk tone always punishing me for something I didn't entirely understand.

The answer would be, I supposed, until my

teacher breathed his last breath. I could not say those words out loud, so I asked her about her son. It's agony to give birth, she replied. Her body was still torn and bruised, they thought she would die, so many stitches, so much blood, and now her breasts were swollen with milk. Even though her son was on formula, the milk kept coming. She pointed to her damp blouse, but I was looking at the four jewelled wings of the dragonfly brooch pinned to her collar.

28

Elsa, Arthur said, where are you?

I'm in Ipswich, I replied.

He closed his eyes.

I'm in Ipswich on the day you came to hear me play the Bösendorfer.

Yes, he whispered.

You said that if you were to teach me, you would take me far away from my life as I knew it so far.

I told you the truth.

Why was I taken away from her?

Where are you, Elsa?

Do you mean geographically?

He pointed to his head and then his heart.

Oh, the head.

So you have not read the documents?

It was as if he were implying my heart would be broken if I read the documents. His lips were moving. I leaned in closer to hear him.

And then closer.

If you are not you, who?

That night I sat alone at the bar with the blaring television. After a couple of beers, I began to cry. It was a shock to weep so loudly through a commercial for fabric softener. The man who owned the bar continued watching television. He didn't seem to mind that his only customer was sobbing. The fabric softener apparently had flowers of gardenia in it. White flowers floated across the screen and landed in the upturned palm of a woman caressing her face with a towel.

If you are not you, who?

If she was not there, where?

The woman who had bought the horses was far away, somewhere else. And then she came through. Her voice was soft and clear, like water trickling over stones on a shallow riverbed.

Maybe you know.
  Maybe I know what?
  That she was there.

Andrew wanted to go to the beach again the next morning. It seemed as if I had no choice but to accompany him. He spent most of the time talking to the man from Somalia who drew the price of his goods with his finger in the sand. It was too early for the Maestrale to come in, but it seemed to have arrived.

  You are a sorceress, Andrew said to me. You're lifting the waves and will drown us all.

  I ran into the turbulent sea. At first I tried diving through the waves. As the current pulled me out, I could not get my breath back before the next one crashed over my head. Two surfers walking the beach with their boards tucked under their arms had obviously decided not to get in. If I wanted to swim back to shore, I was going to have to use all my strength to get there.

Maybe you don't want to.
Maybe I don't want to what?
Swim back to death and the documents.

She was there again, with me, as I spluttered and gasped.

Andrew called out to me. He had bought two rolls of cloth from the Somalian farmer. He held them above his head, waving them in my direction. I heard him shouting and then his voice was lost to the wind. When I emerged from the wild sea, he showed me how to arrange the cotton material over my body to stop the sand whipping my skin and eyes. He wrapped the cloth around himself too. We looked like nomads as we walked across the dunes. Separate but together. Walking forwards to deaf.

In the car, Andrew seemed to be in a friendlier mood.

I am pleased to have you here.

What will you do with Arthur's house? I asked him.

Sell it. I need funds for when I become an old codger.

As we drove through the black and charred forest, Andrew told me he was once a gambler. He had lost everything. But it was the gambling instinct that had made him take a risk with loving Arthur. To his amazement, Arthur had taken a risk on him. Love was the adrenalin, the addiction, it was like a slot machine, you put the coins in and a poet of twentieth-century music was the jackpot. Yet Arthur would not share a bank account. Not at all. After all, he had a child to support. Andrew glanced angrily at me. His money, he said, is your money. He has taken his responsibility for you very seriously. But you have not taken your responsibility for him seriously.

This was true.

You won't read the documents?

I shook my head.

Well, to save Arthur's breath I should tell you.

No, don't do that.

Elsa, you are wearing Arthur out.

He was driving fast now, as if he feared I would open the door and jump out of the car. If I had stayed in the sea, I would never have to read the documents. I pulled the cotton sheet over my head.

You have more or less told Arthur everything there is to know, he said.

Yes, she was his student.

His hands on the steering wheel. His foot on the gas.

Her neighbours took you in. And then Arthur stepped up. He likes to collect lost souls, does Arthur. We don't have to be geniuses to get his attention.

That night I lay on the bed in my sweltering room and read the documents.

Name: Baby girl.

The mosquitoes. The whir of the fan next to my bed. Sand in my nostrils and ears. My body. Naked. Long and lean. The jewel in my belly button. Seaweed in my blue hair. There was nothing I could do to enchant her. She had not even named me. I had been given up by my birth mother as soon as I was born. It was her address that pierced me the most. There was a field between us for the first six years of my life.

29

I knew she was there, but I didn't want to scare her. I felt that with great urgency. I thought I saw her one Tuesday leaning against a stone wall on the border between two fields. The wall had a gap in it that had not yet been filled. The farmer did not have the time or money to repair the walls and sometimes replaced them with barbed-wire fences. I had crawled under the wire of one of those fences to get to the wall. Her skirt was knotted around her hips, as if the zip had broken. She was naked from the waist up. Her back was pushed against the wall, her eyes were closed. She stood very still. A dragonfly hovered above her head like a turquoise needle with wings. When it flew past her face, she opened her eyes.

*

She knew I was there, but she refused to look in my direction.

I wondered if she might be ashamed of me.

I was ashamed of her. I thought she was a mad person, naked from the waist up. It stoked the fire of my secret fear that my mother might be unhinged. That she had done something wrong to lose me. And then I saw that she was sun-bathing. The stone wall was golden. Sunlit. The stones must have been warm against her skin.

30

The woman who ran the embroidery school had made seven dresses to sell at the market on the edge of town. They hung on a portable rail. One of them was cut from white silk, similar to the dress my double had worn when she ran away from me in Paris. White like chalk. The chalk that made the shapes of the alphabet on the blackboard at school. I had listened to the sounds in words and how sounds blend. I was required to raise my pointing finger and trace around the letter *A* for *Ann*. My foster-parents had named me.

Embroidered on the skirt were tiny wild flowers. The wind lifted it like a flag, perhaps a white flag of surrender. Marielle asked if I would like to try it on. She would reduce the price, she said, there was a small tear under the arm, she had no time to mend it before market day. I felt close to both my double and my mother in the delicate dress. Sleeveless, flowing, torn.

She had lived in the broken-down cottage at the end of the field of my childhood home. It was the forbidden pasture. Not once had I asked who lived there. Perhaps I did not want to know the answer to that question. It would float through all of time.

Marielle began to fold the dress in tissue paper.

She told me the silk was from the Veneto.

The words in the document. The official language.

Weight. Height. Eye colour.

Father: Unknown.

Nowhere did the documents describe how her piano was pulled by the horses from her place to my place. I touched it and it touched me back. The Bösendorfer grand. We would never let go of each other, that was my pact with her piano. I felt my mother's presence every day and night. Someone who was unknown to me, but who was nevertheless listening very attentively. I could not see her clearly, but I was intensely feeling her. She was supposed to belong to me. To the church. To my unknown father. To fabric conditioner with gardenias in it. She was twenty when she gave birth and we all had our hands on her. If she belonged to music, she had sent the only thing she wanted, her last desire for herself, to me. I paid for the dress and walked around town. Eventually I stopped at a café and ate the dish of the day, which was called lorighittas, meaning braided pasta. I was still furious with her. The whole world was furious with her. Except for Arthur. He had never judged her. Let her be. Let her find the moon. He had not pointed his pointing finger in her direction. Instead, he had tried to help his student. I understood that his silence, when I eventually began to ask questions about her, was to encourage me to make something of her that was my own. After all, she had already been written by everyone else.

Age: 20.

31

I told Arthur I had read the documents.

My teacher reached for my hand.

I was wanting, he said in his new tiny voice. I took advantage of your need for family. I worked you too hard, I was merciless.

Yes, I said.

A motorbike revved up outside the window. I could hear mosquitoes close to my ear. The frantic beating of their wings. The wailing high sound. The sound of my mother's silence in the cottage opposite my childhood house. Somehow, I had known. She heard me play. My fingers were speaking to her every day.

All the same, I said.

I was trying to tell him I loved him. But the words would not come out of the wild sea.

Every time I tried to haul them to shore, a wave tumbled and crashed and silenced them.

All the same, it's not exactly the same old story.

He knew I was referring to the documents.

Really? He seemed surprised. Why do you say that?

She didn't drown herself in the River Orwell. She sent me her piano.

I see, he murmured.

All the same, you are the only parent who claimed me. And the only father I ever wanted.

Arthur looked surprised.

Perhaps he expected me to say he was the best teacher in the world. His eyelids quivered for a few seconds. In a way he looked disappointed, as if his vanity had been offended.

Play for me, Arthur whispered, play the Rach.

Lit by the glow of the pink-fringed lampshade, I played all night on the ivory keys, while Arthur, propped up on a pile of old pillows, listened with his eyes wide open. This is where we were. Here. Forever entwined in music. The scorpion rug and lamp and Steinway transplanted from our home in Richmond to Sardinia. My insured hands were scratched, blistered, brown from the relentless sun of Sardinia. I started with Rach's tolling bells in Piano Concerto No. 2 and moved on to other musical thoughts and preoccupations. As the feral cats hissed and an ambulance belted through town, I cancelled everything I thought I was and let in everything else that came to me. It was a kind of memorial, not just for my father-teacher, but for the virtuoso he had created.

And I thought of my double in Athens and Paris as I played. Like my mother, she was listening very attentively. What I saw were the pink flowers growing by the Acropolis. I let them enter the music. They had taken me back to another ancient history. To the table-cloths and toast and the blackberry bushes of the first six years with my foster-parents, to the chickens in the garden and the roses falling away from the wall. They had tried to give me a home. To the day Arthur told me he could not teach Ann, but he could teach Elsa, and how my talent would lift me to a bigger home if I wanted it. He meant a home in art. It turned out that I did want it. There were enough rooms in that home for the loneliness that engulfed me all the time, the rage that was always there. I heard the breath of the panting horses that sweltering August, felt the longing for what they were pulling towards me, closer, closer, dragging my mother to me across the parched field under the Suffolk sky. She did not want to be found. The horses delivered her piano instead.

Leave her to solitude. Let her be. Let her find the moon.

I found her in music, alone, sunbathing against the ruins of the stone wall. Perhaps she did not find the moon, but she did find the sun. A dragonfly hovers near her face. She opens her eyes and fleetingly looks at me. I look at her. I gaze at her for all of time. The oldest story will never give me shelter from that gaze, transmitting at this moment to the tips of my fingers and the curve of my thumbs on the ivory keys.

Arthur lay on the bed with his arms folded.

Think of all the beautiful things you can do now, he whispered.

32

I spent the next day lying in the hammock under the parched grapevines. At five in the afternoon Arthur asked for a Bénédictine. I found it for him in the supermarket that night. It was a miracle to chance upon one dusty bottle on the shelf. A miracle. A miracle. The label on the bottle told us it was made from flowers, herbs, roots and berries. He took a tiny sip.

You have your mother's height, he said. I was always struck by her profile when she played. Yet when she took her bow, before a performance, and after it, she stared at her feet.

I was kneeling by his bed, close to his face so I could hear him.

I am a very short person, he said, and turned

his head towards me, as if to confirm this was true.

Yes, I said.

Therefore, he replied, I have always felt the ground beneath my feet, but for anatomical reasons I have had to look upwards, otherwise I would only see my feet. You can go a long way just looking at your feet, but the Pope will never scream and the *Mona Lisa* will never wear a moustache.

He lifted his emaciated left arm towards the blades of the fan whirling above him on the ceiling.

And look at where we are now.

Again he turned towards me.

Where are we now?

Well, he said. I notice that you take a deep bow, before and after a performance. You bend from the waist. And up again to face the audience. Your arms leave your side and stretch outwards to gather them in.

He lifted his little finger and placed it on the scab at the corner of his mouth.

When they unveil my statue at various

conservatoires, he whispered, you can be sure they will have saved money on the quantity of marble or bronze needed to replicate the little Maestro. I will be a cheap date.

Andrew must have heard us both laughing. He walked into the room and asked if Arthur was drunk. Arthur raised his glass of Bénédictine in a salute to him. His thoughts began to wander towards the wife of Mahler. Alma Mahler apparently drank a whole bottle of Bénédictine every day. At one point he announced to us both, My dears, the Ninth Symphony of Beethoven seems to have gone down very well and the autograph hunters have been predatory.

In the morning when Andrew walked into my room without knocking I knew Arthur had died.

His belief in me has been a strong presence in my life, Andrew said.

I could say the same, I replied.

I suppose you are going to return to London and sell Arthur's house?

No. Paris.

It was my house. He wanted my house. He wanted to smash into it like a bailiff. To pay him back for something I did not understand.

I followed him into the garden. He started to unwind the hosepipe.

Andrew, I said, I'm sorry I was not here when Arthur was sick and you needed help.

He turned his back on me. I could hear him crying as he pointed the hose at the thirsty vines.

33

PARIS, AUGUST

I had left my winter coat in the Express dry-cleaners on Rue des Carmes nine months ago. At that time, I was pale and blue, now I was tanned and the blue was fading. It was a hot day to be wearing the trilby hat. A queue had gathered outside the dry-cleaners. It seemed that a customer had brought a hotel's worth of sheets to be cleaned. The woman behind the till was examining each of them before she accepted the job.

I gazed up the hill at the white dome of the Panthéon. Amongst those buried inside it were Victor Hugo, Émile Zola, Voltaire. There was some discussion about where Arthur should be buried, but it would probably be in Sardinia. Andrew wanted to grow flowers on his grave. It was odd because Arthur Goldstein was a public person, he did not belong to Andrew alone. There would be requests for him to be buried next to the acclaimed and famous in Highgate Cemetery or Père Lachaise. He'd taught many international students who were now distinguished musicians. They would want to pay their respects at his graveside. Perhaps Arthur's last climb was to submit to ordinary, everyday love.

A woman had parked her electric scooter outside the dry-cleaners. A large white parrot sat perched between the handlebars. It seemed to know we would be in the queue until sunset. After a while it tucked its head under its wing and dozed off in the sunshine. I began to feel dizzy, so I left the queue and wandered off down a side street.

The world was spinning slowly in this time of bereavement. At night, when I gazed at the stars above Notre-Dame, I had to accept that Arthur had fallen out of the world. I was hungry all the time, yet could not eat anything at all. I found myself standing next to a boulangerie opposite an imposing stone church. A sign told me this church had originally been built on a field of thistles in the thirteenth century. Standing outside the boulangerie, looking in, I could see about nine bees had settled on the white sugar balls that coated the loaves of brioche arranged on a shelf by the window. When the assistant reached for a brioche, she was wearing plastic gloves. I watched the bees while the sun beat down on my shoulders. They were slow, dazed, satiated as they sucked the sugar. Perhaps these bees had mapped the memory of the thistle field in the thirteenth century. They had made their way to this particular foraging site, only to discover it was no longer there. In the same way, I had mapped the memory of the horses in Ipswich and it had surfaced in Athens, transmitted to me by a stall of mechanical animals powered by batteries. I took a sip of water from the warm plastic bottle in my hand. Someone tapped my shoulder.

*

I could see her reflection in the window as I gazed at the bees and brioche. The woman who had bought the horses was standing behind me in a yellow halter-neck dress. Our bodies morphed together into one shadow: four arms, two heads. I would have to turn around and face her, she who might be myself, but who was definitely herself.

One, two, three.

I've read the obituaries, she said. You are in all of them.

Yes, my teacher died, I replied.

She nodded. He said you were his last student. A gift in his old age. Apparently, your middle name is Miracle. Elsa M. Anderson.

I stared over her shoulder and considered running away, as she had first done.

Look, she said, I don't mind about the hat.

Two women on the street were pointing at me.

They've read the obituaries too, she said. Your photo is in all of them. Now they know your middle name is Miracle, they believe that sick people can be cured by touching your foot.

I don't know what to do, I replied.

We decided to meet at Café de Flore the next morning.

The hot weather had broken and it was raining. It took me two hours to get dressed. There was no cold water in the shower of the hotel's bathroom. It came out scalding hot, like Nietzsche's relationship with Wagner, then eventually changed to something cooler. I brushed out my hair one hundred times, spent an hour pinning it up. The Sardinian sun had made my green eyes brighter. Maybe not so much lustrous as lachrymose. I put balm on my lips and hoop earrings in my ears, laced up my sneakers. Last of all, I slipped into the chalky-white silk dress I had bought in Italy and I put on the trilby hat. It had stopped raining.

She was waiting for me at a table on the terrace of Flore.

Her green raincoat was wet. Perhaps she had set off early and been caught in the rainstorm.

Hello, Queen, she said, want to keep me company?

I sat down next to her. We were sitting in

the front row of tables and chairs, side by side, facing Boulevard Saint-Germain. Under her green coat I glimpsed the same pleated white silk dress she had worn on the day I first saw her in Paris. There were two tiny holes in the collar. Moths, she said, they like silk. Our conversation over three countries in Europe had mostly taken in what was behind us, the past, but now I was sitting alongside her in the present.

I know all about you, she said.

What do you know?

There was something in my hand. The tube of orange-flower hand cream I had bought on the day she walked past me at Flore.

I unscrewed the lid and started to rub it into my fingers.

You were a famous pianist, she said. And then you lost it.

Yes.

And now you have lost your teacher too.

I passed her the hand cream. She squeezed a few drops on to her left wrist.

You've been following me around, I challenged her.

The traffic was the same as usual. Choked.

You have to take care of your hands, she said.

What were you doing in Green Lanes, London?

I was never in London.

I told her how I thought I had seen her peering at the gold wedding jewellery in the shops, then walking past the gözleme and kebab places and waiting outside the bakery Yasar Halim.

She shook her head.

But you were in Athens when I was there?

Yes.

And you bought the horses.

Yes.

The waiter interrupted us. We would like two glasses of Perrier-menthe, she told him in her voice of hot stones.

You must be missing your teacher?

I regret not showing him around Athens and Paris before he was too old and lame to walk on his own.

She lowered her head.

I have been walking him around for you, she said.

Who?

Your teacher. He liked the Cycladic Art Museum in Athens and had an affinity with the Greek people. In Paris he admired the bridges and the sheep's cheese with cassis berries.

You're the crazy one, I laughed. You're trying to spook me. My teacher would never eat sheep's cheese with cassis berries. His favourite dish was mashed potato. Who was the old man with you?

Oh, she smiled, taking out a box of cigars from her raincoat pocket. He is my father.

We both lit a cigar with the gold lighter I had found the night I swam away from Tomas on Love Bay and brought with me to death in Sardinia.

You need an even burn, she said. Rotate the outside edges and move the flame towards the centre.

The waiter brought our Perrier-menthe and a small bowl of potato crisps. We sat in silence, smoking in the front row of Flore. Our hands smelled of orange blossom. She had olive skin and brown eyes. Her accent was not English.

Small birds hopped on to our table and pecked at the crisps. I was still wearing her hat. After a while I noticed that my hand was resting on her left shoulder.

It's nice, she said, to be sitting with a miracle.

It was as if we had swum to the island I had dreamed up for us after all.

Or perhaps it was a bay.

She calmed me.

She was like the corner of a room.

She held the gold lighter tight in her hand.

A man in his fifties stopped at our table. He carried a large blue-and-red checked bag with a zip, made from strong plastic. If he was homeless, he had taken care of himself. He was shaved and the skin on his face was radiant, his pink shirt clean and ironed.

He said he was from Singapore and he had been researching medicine ever since his father became ill. In his bag he had prepared multiple copies of the papers that were all of his life's research. He asked if we would like to read his documents. It seemed he wanted us to read them, but it was not a straightforward exchange. We gave him twenty euro and, though he hadn't asked for money, he accepted it gracefully.

Please wait, he said, he would need to organize the documents in his bag. He kneeled down by our table and started to assemble various pages of A4 paper. The bag was stacked with multiple photocopies of swirling handwriting, in black ink. He gave me five sheets, checked that they were numbered, thanked us both and walked away.

It seemed from the information on his documents that he was a doctor and could be found at a certain park for consultations between the time of 2.30 and 4.30. This was crossed out with a correction, 4.30 to 5.30, with the name of the nearest Métro stop. He had, he wrote, cured the various maladies of his sick father, who had died ten years ago. Every day he still cried for his father. He wrote about how, when a mother emperor penguin lays her egg, she returns to the sea for two months to feed herself. It is the father's job, he wrote, to keep the egg warm and safe. He will balance the egg on his feet while she is on her journey, protecting it from predators through the cold winter. The father will not be able to eat for two months. When the mother returns, he makes his way to the sea to nourish himself. On page two he wrote about how elephants cry when their family dies and how when they are born their sisters spray sand over their bodies to protect them from the sun. He wrote *I LOVE YOU FOREVER* underneath this information. All the *O*'s were drawn in the shape of hearts. On page three he listed all the subjects in the sciences he had studied. There were 107 of them, all numbered, from anatomy to pulmonology, urology to oncology, with interventions in capital letters, *I LOVE YOU VERY VERY MUCH FOREVER!!*

He had read a total of 300,000 scientific papers, he wrote, but most of all, in order to live a healthy life, he recommended sunlight and exercise, to drink hot water, to eat purple vegetables, also garlic and ginger, to eat beef ribs twice a week, to take potassium, magnesium, gold, iron, to run until sweat appears and to have an early night.

His words were different from the words in my documents. Nowhere were the words *I LOVE YOU VERY VERY MUCH FOREVER!!*

Those words are only important if you mean them, she said, relighting the cigar that had gone out while we were reading the papers.

I believe he understands them, I replied.

But to make the *O*'s into hearts – she blew out a wisp of smoke – that's a cheap shot.

The cigar was glowing between her lips.

After a while she plucked it out and let it rest in the ashtray.

I have something for you.

She took a bundle of newspaper out of her bag and placed it on the table. The newspaper was written in the Greek alphabet and I knew the horses lay inside it. I lifted the trilby hat from my head and passed it to her.

She nonchalantly put it on and tipped it over her eyes, as if she had never been parted from it.

It felt as if everything had changed and everything was the same. The roots of the trees under the tarmac of Boulevard Saint-Germain would keep growing. The roots of my hair would keep growing out the blue. The sea levels would keep rising. Two young people standing by the bus stop were kissing. Frantic kissing. As if this devouring of each other was an existential duty. The obligation to keep the life drive going strong when death is our ultimate destiny.

I LOVE YOU VERY VERY MUCH FOREVER. Was it a cheap shot?

Arthur often told me, 'I admire your great strength,' I said.

She wanted to know what he meant.

You already know, I said. You made me tell you across four countries what he meant.

She began to sneeze. And then she coughed for a long time.

Are you feeling unwell?

I'm not sure, she replied.

It occurred to me that what I had transmitted to her, across four countries, was pain.

We were all striding out into the world once again to infect and be infected by each other. If she was my double and I was hers, was it true that she was knowing, I was unknowing, she was sane, I was crazy, she was wise, I was foolish? The air was electric between us, the way we transmitted our feelings to each other as they flowed through our arms, which were touching.

We agreed that whatever happened next in the world, we would still rub conditioner into our hair after we washed it and comb it through to the ends, we would soften our lips with rose, strawberry and cherry scented balm, and though we would be interested to see a wolf perched on a lonely mountain, we liked our household animals to betray their savage nature and live with us in our reality, which was not theirs. They would lie in our laps and let us stroke them through waves of virus, wars, drought and floods and we would try not to transmit our fear to them.

I unwrapped the newspaper and pulled out the horses. Brown and white. It came to me again. The bereft ache of watching the horses carry the piano across the field. Somehow, I had known it was hers. How was it possible to know such a thing? How do we know what we know? The ticket to the dry-cleaners on the Rue des Carmes fell out of my pocket and fluttered towards the pavement.

She bent down and picked it up and she kept it in her hand.

It started to rain, it always rained when she was around, but we did not move from our seats in the front row of Café de Flore. When I pulled the tail up and held the string around the neck of the dancing brown horse, I could fleetingly hear but not grasp the protest that had gripped me that night in the concert hall in Vienna.

I wanted the old world to melt like winter snow.

When I heard my unlikely double say, Elsa, your arms are quite bare in the rain, I could not bring myself to pull the tail down and let go of the magic. My hair was soaked through and she was wearing the hat. After a while, she leaned over, and with her finger on the tail, she stopped the horse.

I was affronted. For the first time since she had appeared in my life, I stared directly into her eyes. She accepted my gaze and I saw something of who she was, rather than who I had imagined her to be. It was not a comfortable moment. Tears flowed downwards and wet her white silk dress.

We should never overestimate a person's strength just because it suits us to do so, she said.

After a while, she suggested we walk together to collect my coat at the dry-cleaners.

As the rain fell softly and lightly on Boulevard Saint-Germain, I told her that on the night of that concert in Vienna, I had ceased to inhabit Rachmaninov's sadness, and dared for a moment to live in our own.

PILLGWENLLY